SLOW BURN

SIERRA CARTWRIGHT

SLOW BURN

Copyright @ 2021 Sierra Cartwright

First E-book Publication: July 2021

Editing by Nicki Richards, What's Your Story Editorial Services

Line Editing by Jennifer Barker

Proofing by Bev Albin, ELF, Cassie Hess-Dean

Layout Design by Once Upon an Alpha

Cover Design by Once Upon an Alpha

Photo provided by Depositphotos.com

Promotion by Once Upon An Alpha, Shannon Hunt

All rights reserved. Except for use in a review, no part of this publication may be reproduced, distributed, or transmitted in any form, or by any means, electronic or mechanical, including photocopying, recording, or by any information storage and retrieval system, without prior written permission of the author.

This is a work of fiction. Names, characters, places, brands, media, and incidents are either the products of the author's imagination or are used fictitiously, and any resemblance to any actual persons, living or dead, is entirely coincidental.

The author acknowledges the trademarked status and trademark owners of various products referenced in this work of fiction. The publication/use of these trademarks is not authorized, associated with, or sponsored by the trademark owners.

Adult Reading Material

Disclaimer: This work of fiction is for mature (18+) audiences only and contains strong sexual content and situations.

It is a standalone with my guarantee of satisfying happily ever after.

All rights reserved.

DEDICATION

For Cyndi. I'm so glad we're friends. Thanks for the conversations, the support, and most of all, the fun and laughter. You make my life brighter.

CHAPTER ONE

"What do you see?"
Makenna jumped, sending diet soda over the rim of her glass to splash on the polished hardwood floor. The question, unexpectedly sexy and growly against her ear, rocketed sparks of desire down her spine.

Although they'd never been introduced, she'd recognize his commanding baritone anywhere. For at least a year, Zachary Denning had starred in her dreams and strolled through her fantasies.

The renowned Dominant was ridiculously rich, movie-star handsome, a battlefield hero…and a notorious heart-breaker. Master Zachary could have any woman on the planet, and from what she'd witnessed—tonight even—fans clamored for his attention.

So why are you talking to me?
"I didn't mean to frighten you."
She started to turn, but he clamped his strong hands on her shoulders, igniting a firestorm inside her.
"No. Please. Stay where you are."

Her pulse skittered, and her breath caught. Did he have any idea how intoxicating his effect was on her?

"That scene has you fascinated."

Since she was momentarily speechless, she settled for nodding.

Every few months, she and her friends from a businesswomen's group attended a play party here at the home of Las Vegas's hottest legal eagles, Diana and Alcott Hewitt.

Not only were the couple partners at the law firm bearing their name, but they owned one of the city's most unique properties—a house that was over twenty thousand square feet with grounds that sprawled over three large lots. The U-shaped home had an amazing courtyard complete with lush tropical foliage and a swimming pool with attached hot tub. Beyond it was a dramatic and rather noisy waterfall. And for clandestine meetings, a grotto was tucked away in the darkest recesses of the garden.

This evening, Makenna stood in front of her favorite place, an observation room, complete with one-way glass. The hot BDSM scene transpiring between her hosts held her riveted. That was the only explanation possible for not noticing Master Zachary's arrival.

"Tell me what you see." It was his second prompt, and command laced his request, compelling an obedience she'd never before experienced.

Unnerved by the billionaire as much as her own response to him, she cleared her throat. "I was about to move on."

"Were you?" His tone was warm, with an underlying mocking note. He'd caught her in a lie and called it out.

Impossibly he moved in closer. She imagined the abrasive rub of his pants against the bare skin of her legs.

Master Zachary had a reputation as a considerate Dominant, which meant she could excuse herself and make an escape at any time. Maybe that was why she remained rooted in place.

"You want to watch every moment until the very end." He slid the words into her ear, his breath warm on her already heated skin. "That's why you're here, isn't it?"

In a rush, she exhaled the painful admission. "Yes."

On the other side of the glass, Master Alcott held up a palm. Diana, naked and collared, sank to her knees and lowered her head. Then, in a move both beautiful and practiced, she cupped her breasts, offering them—and herself—to her Dominant.

"Is that what you want? To be in that position?"

Frantically Makenna shook her head. "I'm not much of a submissive." But if she were, it would be with Master Zachary. He was blessed by the gods with an exquisite body.

"You're not much of a submissive?" A gentle tease roughened his question. "You haven't moved from this place for at least ten minutes."

Which meant he'd been watching her. Had he noticed the way she squirmed when Master Alcott stripped his wife? "Ah...I find it interesting." Makenna cleared her throat. "A curiosity."

"Are you aroused?"

"What?" Heat rushed through her. She was glad he couldn't see the way excitement vanquished her shock.

"Is your pussy wet?"

Oh my God. Embarrassment clogged her throat.

"Be brave."

She couldn't.

"Take a chance. For me."

Because his order was as compelling as it was nonnegotiable, she nodded.

"I'd like to hear the words."

"Yes." Could she do this? Could she not? "I'm wet."

"That pleases me immensely. Yet you hesitated. What are you afraid of?"

"I'm an event planner. I deal with brides and demanding C-types all day long. Nothing scares me." She tried for an air of lightness she didn't feel.

"There are things in this world that are absolutely terrifying."

Of course he would know. She'd read an article about his exploits in her favorite gossip magazine, *Scandalicious*. Though he was from a wealthy background, all the Denning men were expected to serve their country. He'd graduated from a military academy and served heroically in battle before joining the family business. How they made their money, she had no idea. But she'd heard plenty of whispers.

He eased closer, rocketing a response through her and forcing her to admit she was afraid of something. *Him.*

In front of them, Master Alcott took a bit gag down from the wall. His obedient wife continued to stare at him and, without being told, opened her mouth. He placed the gag between her teeth, checked it for fit, then buckled the strap tightly behind her head.

At the sight of Diana's compliance, a bizarre buzzing scrambled around Makenna's ears.

"Describe the scene to me."

Like a moment ago, his command was absolute. Zachary Denning was a man accustomed to being obeyed. The problem was, until now, even though she had her private daydreams, she wasn't a woman accustomed to being told what to do.

"I'm waiting."

This surreal experience was giving her the opportunity to live out her fantasies, if only for the moment. Despite a rush of nervousness, she spoke. "Master Alcott is helping Diana to stand." Makenna tightened her fingers around her glass.

"Now she's walking to the center of the room where there's a massage type of table."

"Keep going."

Is this really happening? "She's bending at the waist, and he's securing her wrists to the far end of the table."

"So she can't move?"

Makenna squirmed. "Not much."

"So theoretically Master Alcott can do whatever he wants to her?"

A shiver rippled through her. "Yes."

"And since she's gagged, she can't say anything. She can't beg for mercy or protest in any way."

Words failed her.

"Do you wonder what it might be like to be in there? To be completely helpless to your Dominant's whims? To have others watching you?"

Her mouth dried. She took a sip of the soda, trying to ignore the fact that her hand was shaking. "Of course not. I've already told you I'm not submissive."

His soft chuckle was more of a scoff. "And your reactions tell a different story. Your breathing." He stroked a finger down the side of her throat. "The fluttering here." He pressed a thumb against her pulse.

If he hadn't kept one hand clamped on her shoulder, she would have fled.

"You haven't told me to go to hell."

Because foolishly she wanted this.

"Let me take your drink, Makenna."

Her pulse skipped a beat, then slammed the next dozen together. "How do you know who I am?" Maybe she should have selected a scene name to hide her identity, though she suspected he would dig through as many layers as it took to discover the information he wanted.

"I make it my business to know all of Diana and Alcott's guests, particularly the beautiful ones."

Beautiful? Not at all, and especially not when compared to the women he was known to date. Despite eating more lettuce than a rabbit, skipping chocolate for long enough to bankrupt Switzerland, and sweating at the gym three times a week, she had bulges and ripples everywhere. "I'm afraid you have the wrong person."

"Be assured, I don't."

What game are you playing?

With a strength that gave her no chance to run, he turned her to face him. For a moment, he stroked her shoulders, so sensually that her insides began to unravel. Then, when he tightened his fingers again, she tipped back her head to meet his gaze.

This close, he made her tremble.

He wore black trousers rather than leather pants or jeans. Light winked off the masculine gold ring and expensive watch that he wore. A tailored white dress shirt conformed to his body, emphasizing the athletic cut and definition of his well-honed biceps. Expensive shoes added an inch or two to his height, not that he needed it. He was already over six feet tall, towering over her, even in her heels.

His strong jaw was set in a firm line. But his eyes grabbed her attention. They were dark and deep—a blue-gray like the Atlantic during a tumultuous storm. Tiny grooves were carved next to them. Master Zachary had clearly seen more of life than she ever would, and it gave him an air of confidence, of mastery. No matter how hard she tried, she couldn't bear to look away from the intensity that suddenly blazed in his expression.

At that moment, a male server wearing tight black slacks and a red bowtie approached.

Master Zachary finally released her to take her glass.

After placing it on the tray, he snagged a napkin to wipe up her earlier spill.

His thoughtfulness surprised her.

When they were alone once more, he took a slight step back and swept his gaze over her. If what her ex-boyfriend said was true, Master Zachary was cataloging her numerous flaws.

"Gorgeous. Simply gorgeous."

She blinked at his reaction.

"Now, I'd like your legs shoulder width apart."

She had no idea what he had in mind, but if she offered him the control he wanted, she would be changed forever.

"You're hesitating. And again, you haven't told me to go to hell."

Master Zachary's presence was as undeniable as it was compelling.

"Courage, Makenna. Why not seize the moment?"

With a shaky breath, she did as he'd instructed, terribly aware of how short her skirt was.

"You follow directions well. You please me."

His approval weakened her knees. It had been so, so long...

"Now face the scene again."

As before, he placed his hands on her shoulders, but this time, his grip was possessive.

While they watched, Master Alcott slid his hand between Diana's legs. The woman arched her back, as if silently asking for more.

"Please continue your narration."

"Master Alcott seems to be stroking Diana's..." Makenna trailed off. "Her clit."

"And does she seem to be enjoying it?"

"Yes." As much as possible, Diana lifted her body, seemingly begging for her Master's touch. Makenna couldn't help but picture herself in Diana's place, with Zachary's strong fingers parting her labia.

Master Alcott moved away. Diana's hips swayed side to side gently and invitingly.

"What is he doing?" Master Zachary asked.

"Ah..." Her eyes widened. "He's getting... Oh my God." Little points of metal winked in the overhead lights. "Vampire gloves."

"Have you ever used them?"

She shook her head. Then she revealed more than she intended. "I haven't experienced most things related to BDSM." Truth was, while she yearned for more, she lacked the courage.

"And are you curious?"

"About the gloves in particular?" She shivered as Master Alcott checked the fit and flexed his fingers. "No. They terrify me."

"I can understand that. Yet the simultaneous dance of pain and pleasure can be addictive."

The image of Master Zachary exploring her body sashayed through her mind.

Intently focused, Master Alcott traced the little spikes up the outsides of his wife's thighs, then the insides, forcing her to rise onto her toes.

Diana turned her head to the side, so Makenna could read her expression. As the Dominant neared his submissive's pussy, she closed her eyes.

Instead of touching her most intimate place, he grabbed hold of her buttocks and squeezed.

Makenna yelped.

Master Zachary chuckled. "Sympathy reaction?"

"That had to hurt."

"Most likely."

Master Alcott said something inaudible before uncurling

his fingers to spank the tops of Diana's thighs. Though Makenna winced, the submissive wore a soft smile.

"He knows what she likes and ensures she receives it."

When Master Alcott again traced his way up the insides of her thighs, Diana parted her legs as far as her restraints allowed, giving herself over to her Dominant. She didn't pull away when he reached her apex.

"Notice the way he's taking in every one of her responses."

To Makenna this was about far more than BDSM. Submitting would mean she trusted a man to keep her best interests at the forefront, something she'd never experienced.

Diana wiggled her ass in invitation, and her Dominant removed his gloves, then picked up a serious-looking broad leather paddle and used it on the places he'd scratched.

Desire drove Makenna out of her mind, and she whimpered, even though she tried to hold it back.

"Have you ever been spanked like that?"

Tiny shakes overtook her. "I've never been spanked at all."

"Would you like a taste?"

God. Yes. "I…"

"Do you have a safe word?"

Though she'd never needed one, this was something she was familiar with. "Red."

"And green to let me know you're okay?"

Driven by the response unfurling in her, she nodded.

"Yellow to slow down?"

At this moment, she couldn't imagine ever wanting to say that.

"Tell me what you want."

No one was near, and she was fully dressed. "Green."

"Very good." Master Zachary slid his forearm in front of her. "You can brace yourself on me."

Before she could respond, he squeezed her right buttock,

and she sighed. It had been so long, and his touch, even through her clothing, made her delirious.

"I smell your arousal." His statement was a silken scandal, unraveling her resistance.

Firm, but not too hard, he delivered a single swat.

"Ohh."

"Green?"

She nodded.

"Remove your panties for me?"

Shock froze her vocal cords.

A primal part of her brain recognized that he was forcing her to be part of the experience.

He didn't press her again. Instead, he remained silent, allowing her the space to make a decision.

This was mortifying. If she took them off, he'd know what size they were. One time, she'd accidentally left a pair in the dryer, and her ex had picked them out, then brought them to her and mentioned that he'd had no idea she was that big.

She wasn't sure she could endure that kind of embarrassment ever again.

"Makenna?"

"I, uh…" Maybe it was better he know all her flaws from the beginning. Not that it mattered. After tonight, she'd never have the opportunity to be with him again.

With a sigh, she used his arm for balance as she removed the bikini-cut underwear.

"Perfect. Now give them to me."

Unable to help herself, she turned as much as possible, hoping to read his expression. The only thing visible was the cold, hard set of his jaw. "You're serious?"

"I'm not known for my sense of humor when giving my submissive a command."

She shuddered. Though they'd been together less than

five minutes, and he'd barely touched her, her mind already spun out of control.

"Your obedience would give me great pleasure." His growly, gravelly, turned-on voice was persuasive as fuck.

With a sigh of resignation, she crouched to scoop up the lace and satin.

"Thank you." He plucked the material from her nerveless fingers and tucked his prize into his pocket. "I'll reward you with several spanks."

Reward? Before she could form the question, he slipped his arm back into place and kept his promise, four times in quick succession.

Then he went on, delivering dozens more, matching the cadence of the ones that Diana was receiving.

Each stroke was hard but dulled by the material that covered her skin. She loved the way he curved his fingers into her, firmly and possessively.

It was mesmerizing and seductive, leaving her dizzy and hungry.

When he finished, Makenna jerked, but he was there, tightening his hold, offering support.

"How was that?"

Breath constricted in her chest. "I'm not entirely sure."

"Can you try to explain?"

Makenna scowled. How was she supposed to answer him? She dug deep in order to understand her own reaction. "It hurt. But it went away fast. And it was only one…"

"Ass cheek?" The suggested words, fed softly into her ear, were light, despite the fact that he said he wasn't known to joke around. "And you want to have a longer, more authentic experience?"

In front of her, the paddling continued. Diana's eyes were closed, and her breaths were long and relaxed.

"Wondering what it might be like to be as euphoric as Diana?"

Because her back was to him, she found an honesty she hadn't with any other man. "Yes."

"Good. Because I want to give you exactly that. And for what I have in mind, we need a little more privacy."

Run.

"Accompany me to the grotto."

She couldn't go any further with him. If she did, she might fall off an emotional cliff, never to recover. "I'm not your type, Master Zachary."

"On the contrary. You absolutely are." He brushed aside a long lock of her blonde hair. "Stunning." Then he placed a gentle kiss on the side of her neck. "Curvy."

That was a kind word, unlike the one her ex had used to describe her.

"Inexperienced yet interested."

Maybe the fact that she hadn't fawned all over him was the appeal. But to her, this was no game. "And you want to be the one to corrupt me?"

"In every way I can think of. And ruin you for every other man."

As if he hadn't already. "That's quite…egotistical."

"Not in the least."

Even though Master Alcott continued to spank his wife, he moved his free hand between her legs to masturbate her.

The peaceful expression on her face vanished, and she bucked wildly, Diana arched toward her Dominant. He rubbed her even harder. Seconds later, she went still before collapsing with a gentle shudder.

Master Alcott faced the glass and smiled, then pressed a button to close the blinds, effectively ending the scene. There was no longer any reason for Master Zachary to stay with her.

"What will it be, my innocent?"

If Makenna didn't seize this moment, would it ever happen again? Her innate sense of preservation warred with her desire to give herself over to the moment.

When she met his gaze and read promise and urgency, she was lost. Everything he offered, she wanted.

"Are you brave enough to turn yourself over to me for the next hour to see what pleasure awaits you?"

CHAPTER TWO

"Makenna!"

At the exclamation, she looked up to see her friend, Avery, striding toward her, accompanied by her fiancé and Dominant, Master Cole Stewart.

"I won't forget that we have unfinished business." Master Zachary's promise was rich and foreboding.

Fortunately she was saved from replying as Avery swept her into a hug.

The men shook hands, and once again, Master Zachary's ring caught a light beam. This time, two emeralds winked, even more noticeable because a similar flash came from the ring Master Cole wore.

After everyone had exchanged greetings, Masters Zachary and Cole turned slightly for a quiet conversation.

Makenna appreciated seeing her friends as it gave her a hint of normalcy. "I didn't know you were going to be here."

"It was last minute." Avery, with her signature sweep of pink in her blonde hair, glanced toward her future husband before leaning closer to Makenna and lowering her voice. "Master Cole bought this outfit for me." She twirled around.

Avery's short skirt flared out, then settled over her hips with a teasing swish. Her black mesh shirt was formfitting, low-cut, and sexy.

"I love it." And she adored the fact that her friend was radiant.

"He wanted me to save it for our honeymoon, but I was dying to wear it."

"Now he'll have to buy you something else."

"Exactly!" Avery grinned.

"Speaking of your honeymoon...?"

"Finally. Yes. Everything is arranged, thanks to you." Avery exhaled.

"Good." One of her professional acquaintances, Elizabeth Gallagher, had been promoted to a VP position in the Sterling Hotel organization. She was a whiz at securing the high-end accommodations at luxurious resorts.

"We're going to a private island in the Caribbean. We'll have a chef, if we want it, groceries delivered by boat, great sunsets, snorkeling, sunshine. It should be"—Avery glanced at her fiancé, who was still talking to Master Zachary—"memorable."

"Sounds perfect."

"I still have a million details that are keeping me up at night." Avery sighed. "Tell me we're still meeting on Tuesday."

"Wouldn't miss it. We have five o'clock reservations for the martini bar at the Bella Rosa." Though they were friends, Makenna was also Avery's wedding planner, and they liked to combine business with pleasure every chance they had.

"Do you mind if we invite Zara?"

"That would be great." Makenna nodded. "I haven't seen her in a month or so."

"Good. Some girl time will help my stress level. And I want to work my way through the happy hour menu, starting with the Italian Wedding Cake drink." Avery grinned.

"If you love it, we can add it to your cocktail hour menu."

"Something other than wine or beer? I like the idea. Budget? What budget?"

Avery was a numbers whiz, and she watched every penny. But Cole wanted to give her a wedding fit for a princess, and he was willing to foot the bill, much to Avery's consternation. She would have been happy with a small event at one of Las Vegas's wedding chapels or even elopement, but Cole was insistent on everything being first class.

After a resigned shrug, Avery slid a glance toward Master Zachary. "Now tell me about you and Master Dreamboat."

Makenna laughed. Avery was one of the few people who knew about her long-term attraction to the stern Dominant. But Makenna had never expected that he'd actually choose her over the throngs of women who hounded him. "I'm not sure what to say." She sighed. "Or what I'm doing."

"Are you enjoying yourself?"

"More than I thought possible."

"Good." Avery smiled. "And I'm going to want all the details on Tuesday."

"I wouldn't think otherwise." Truthfully Makenna was grateful she knew someone she could share her emotions with. No doubt it was going to take some time to sort through them all.

"If you need me before that, make sure you call. Anytime. Night or day. I mean it."

"Thank you." Makenna gave her friend another quick hug.

The two men—self-assured and gorgeous Dominants—ended their conversation, and Cole lightly touched Avery's shoulder. "If you'll excuse us, I'm anxious to get my future bride to her appointment at the spanking bench."

Avery smiled shyly.

"Shall we?"

"Yes, Sir." Then she gave Makenna a little wave. "Tuesday. *All* the details."

For a moment, Makenna watched the couple walk away. Master Cole placed his palm against the curve of Avery's back in a protective, easy intimacy.

Makenna had never experienced anything similar. Her parents had been cool toward their only child, somewhere between indifferent and aloof. As a result, she'd wrapped her emotions in armor so she didn't get hurt.

"You two are close friends, I assume?"

She shook her head to clear it. Until this moment, she hadn't realized how much she'd missed, and how badly she wanted something like Avery had found.

"Makenna?" he prompted when she didn't answer.

"We met at a women-in-business breakfast group, and a few of us have developed our own circle of friends. I'm her wedding planner."

"Excellent job on the invitations."

She faced him, her lips slightly parted. "You're on the guest list?" What a ridiculous question. The city's elite would be in attendance, including everyone whose address was on Sin City's Billionaire's Row.

"I'll get to see you in action."

Which meant that—no matter what—she would have to see him again. She wasn't sure whether the idea thrilled her or terrified her.

And then it occurred to her. Of course he'd bring a date.

That she wasn't sure she could survive.

"Now that we're alone again, I'd like to revisit our earlier conversation. Are you brave enough to accompany me to the grotto?"

She frowned, considering the question.

It was one thing to have secret fantasies about the Dominant. But the reality was, they were from two different worlds. She'd earned college scholarships. Even at that, she'd worked at a catering company—nights, weekends, and holidays—while attending classes. She'd spent a lot of her life waiting on people like him.

Even though she ran her own company, her clients moved in his social circles—evidenced by the fact that he'd be at Cole and Avery's wedding.

It would be foolish to allow herself to believe she was anything more than a diversion to him. And yet, she didn't indulge in random experiences. She needed to care about someone to sleep with them.

Instead of pressing her for an answer, Master Zachary stood there with his hands clasped behind his back, allowing the silence to expand while he took in her reactions. Surprising her, he never looked away, giving her the gift of his complete attention.

"Just a scene?"

"Everything you want, and nothing more." His voice was as gruff as it was sexy, turning her on.

So why am I hesitating? He wasn't asking her about their future. In fact, he wasn't even suggesting they go out on a date. He was offering to fulfil her fantasies. And if she turned him down, he might never approach her again.

The grotto was a safe place to hide her self-doubts. Since it was remote, it was safe from onlookers. From what she'd heard, the interior was dimly lit, which meant she'd be able to hide her embarrassment as well as her body. "I um…" After clearing the sudden knot of fear from her throat, she nodded. "Yes. I'll go with you."

"I'm honored." His smile was slow and wicked.

No doubt he intended to appear gentlemanly, yet it was

anything but, and the predatory gleam in his eye sent a shiver through her.

"I promise you, it will be an evening you won't forget."

Earlier she'd suggested he was egotistical, and this comment was in the same vein. Yet even after the small taste of a BDSM experience, she was afraid he meant every word.

"My play bag is in the foyer."

Which meant he'd fully intended to scene this evening.

"Walk with me? I'm afraid you'll succumb to your doubts and vanish on me if I leave you alone."

How well he already knew her.

Oftentimes, Tops had their partner walk a little behind them, and she'd noted some wearing leashes. Yet he was behaving as they might at a vanilla event.

"Is the grotto available?" he asked the attendant when they reached the home's foyer.

She glanced at the sign-in log. "Yes, Master Zachary."

"I'd like to book it for an hour."

"Of course, Sir. Will you need your bag?"

"Please."

Less than two minutes later, she returned. The owl embossed on the side caught Makenna's attention.

After thanking the attendant, he extended his hand in front of him, indicating that she should lead the way toward the rear exit. Once there, he leaned over her to open the door and held it for her. Such elegant manners in real life would sweep her off her feet.

The Nevada evening with its hot breeze wrapped around her, sultry and inviting. Her heart quickened as they passed other guests. Within thirty seconds, the music from unseen speakers high in the palm trees became fainter, and the boisterous shouts from attendees splashing in the pool receded.

As they neared the grotto, solar lights dotting the garden provided the only illumination.

"Nervous?"

She glanced over her shoulder.

"Your breaths... I can hear them."

Was there no way to keep secrets from this man?

"You're perfectly safe with me."

Safe? No doubt that meant something different to him than it did to her.

The cavelike grotto structure was sealed shut by two heavy arched wood doors. A metal bolt was in place across both. After sliding it open, he tugged on the handle to allow them entrance.

The cavernous space shocked her.

Despite the outside heat, the grotto was cool. Flickering lanterns hung from the ceiling. Though there was enough light to see by, it wasn't bright, and the dimness created an intimate ambience.

The floor was made from uneven slate-gray flagstone. Numerous pillows, in various sizes, shapes, and colors, were scattered about.

Long lengths of gauzy material were draped along the walls, and for a moment, she was swept away into an Arabian-nights fantasy.

She startled when he sealed them inside and secured a lock for privacy.

"What do you think?"

Against one wall was a low purple bench, and also a shelving unit where Master Zachary stowed his toy bag.

"It's a lot to take in." A Saint Andrew's cross stood near the back of the area, and now that her vision had adjusted to the light, she noticed the gleam of rings—shackles—attached to the walls.

"And it's soundproof."

She turned to stare at him. His arms were folded, and his jaw was set. Never had she seen a man look so Dominant.

"Are you serious?"

"You can cry and scream all you want. No one will save you."

Makenna shivered.

"Would you like to test my words?"

Quickly she shook her head. He'd made it clear he didn't joke.

"Now come to me, my innocent one." He paused. "If you dare." With great deliberation, he unfolded his arms and crooked a finger, beckoning her forward.

On wooden legs, she did as he commanded.

He turned away long enough to grab his bag and place it on the bench. Then he looked at her. "Go ahead and open it. If you're interested in trying out any of my toys, we can. Or we can continue what we started in the house, using my bare hand."

The sound of the zipper was unnaturally loud, bouncing off the stone enclosure.

He had a dizzying array of implements. She'd been around the scene long enough to recognize them. Large and small floggers, paddles, several slappers, an evil-looking tawse, even a single tail. "The whip is a definite no."

"Understood. Off-limits. As for the rest of them?"

The courage she wanted was nowhere around. After sighing, she turned her head to look at him. "I'd like to start with your hand again." Even though it was more personal, which meant her choice was a greater threat to her emotions.

"My preference as well." His smile was the reassurance she needed. "For what happens next, I want to see your body."

Mortification swamped her. *"What?"* The only time she'd been nude with her ex was when the lights were completely off. And this man wanted her to expose her flaws to him.

"Can you do that for me? It's part of the mental preparation for your submission." He plucked at a wayward strand of hair, then curled it around his finger. "You're beautiful, Makenna. You may not see it, but I promise you, I do."

"I—" She'd been about to protest, but instead, stopped herself. He was a charmer, no doubt. Disagreeing with him would beget more arguments.

Nerves swarming through her, she closed her eyes.

"No. Watch me watch you."

She exhaled.

"Look at me." He gave her a moment before adding, "That's your first order." His voice was different, sharper. Uncompromising.

"You don't ask for much, do you?"

"Is that what you want? A man, a Dominant, who will expect nothing from you? Who will allow you to be passive?"

"No." Her whispered admission was painful. That wasn't what she wanted at all. This was the man of her fantasies, of her dreams. No matter what, she would always have this evening to remember. And the more memories, the better.

"Start with your shoes."

Once they were off, she became even more aware of their height difference, how big and powerful he was.

"Keep going."

She drew her shirt up and over her head. But before she could let it fall to the ground, he snagged it in midair and reached over to place it on the bench.

He sucked in a sharp breath. "You're even more gorgeous than I imagined."

This evening, she dressed in a lacy, delicate demi bra that barely contained her voluptuous breasts.

He traced a fingertip from the hollow of her throat downward a couple of inches before pausing. "May I?"

As she nodded, she lowered her head.

"No. Please remember my command. I want your gaze to be locked on me."

"I'm not sure I can do that." She wanted to hide from this, from him. And yet his demand encouraged her to enjoy every moment.

"I'll remind you as often as it takes. But I won't be denied."

Fighting her demons, her slamming heart, she summoned the courage to meet his gaze.

"Good. Your eyes are so expressive, revealing your reactions. And that pleases me." Gently he slid his palms beneath the fabric covering her breasts. Then, his touch warm and firm, he gently squeezed. At the same time, he scraped his thumbnails across her nipples, abrading them. Instantly the tips rose, and she involuntarily groaned.

"Responsive." Master Zachary smiled. "And sensitive." Sincerity flared in his shocking blue eyes.

Her body might be bigger than she wanted, but he made it clear that to him it was perfect. Maybe she could do this after all.

"May I?"

As she nodded, he reached around to unhook her bra. Slowly, as if savoring the moment as much as she was, he eased the straps down her arms.

With perfect precision, taking care of her belongings, he placed the lingerie on top of her shirt.

"How much nipple play do you like? A little? A lot?"

As if he had all the time in the world, he caressed her. He squeezed her nipples, tugging on them until they thickened and elongated; then he lowered his head to suck one into his mouth. He laved it with his tongue, drawing the tight flesh deeper inside his mouth. The swirling, teasing pressure drove her mad. Unsure how to ask for what she wanted, she leaned forward, giving herself, offering herself to him.

"Yeah. That's exactly right. I like my submissives to willingly give me everything I want."

The jarring words crashed her back into reality. That was what she was to him. Another woman in a long line of submissives who lined up to be the object of his desire.

Before she could react, giving voice to her doubts, he sucked her other nipple into his mouth, this time with more pressure, making her cry out. When she might have pulled away, he placed his hand on the middle of her back, holding her steady and preventing escape.

Finally he was done. He sighed deeply and passionately, making her wet, making her moan, making her forget her traitorous thoughts to the point that she wasn't sure she could even remember her own name.

"You're doing great. Surrender to the experience, to the moment, and just let it happen. No past, no future." He smiled, but it didn't make him any less dangerous. "And yes, I do know what I'm asking for and how difficult it is for you. So we'll start with an over-the-knee spanking and go from there?"

That seemed overwhelmingly personal. If she were attached to Saint Andrew's cross, he'd likely be using an implement, which meant there'd be distance between them, and he wouldn't be physically touching her.

With a gentleness that surprised her, he captured her wrist and drew her to the bench where he took a seat. "Ready?"

He offered his support as she lowered herself into place. The position, with her ass in the air, pulled the skirt tight and made it ride up. He placed one arm across her to hold her in place and then angled his thighs to move her closer to him. Since he'd thrown her off-balance, she pressed her fingertips to the floor for stability.

"That's better." He captured the hem of her skirt and drew it up over her buttocks. "So very spankable."

She wished she could accept his compliment without embarrassment.

"Surrender to the experience. The more you relax, the easier this will be, and the more you'll enjoy it."

"That's totally impossible."

"It's not. Take a breath." With small, gentle motions, he massaged her upper thighs.

For a moment she tensed, but he continued to soothe her.

"I recognize that trust is difficult. But I promise you that I will do everything it takes to earn it. I see you, Makenna, and I appreciate every single thing about you."

"All my flaws, you mean?" Maybe it was a good thing she was facedown; at least this way she could hide her humiliation.

"I see a woman who has the type of curves that men fantasize about. That I fantasize about. You're womanly."

Maybe it was from the lack of oxygen going to her brain, or from his featherlight caresses and reassuring words, but she began to relax.

"Keep breathing and let go."

She exhaled with a shudder.

"That's perfect. May I have your permission to touch your pussy?"

He was stroking everywhere, and arousal made her resistance collapse. "Yes." It was more a plea than permission.

With maddening lightness, he brushed across her clitoris, igniting raw feminine hunger.

Before bringing her to completion, he resumed spanking her, first with love taps and then increasing the intensity.

"Remember to breathe." He covered her exposed skin from the tops and insides of her thighs to her lower buttocks. And then the fleshier parts.

If he inflicted any pain, she didn't register it. Her entire body was heated, feverish. Then when she wasn't sure she could take any more, he pressed his thumb against her clit and slid two fingers inside her.

"So wet. So damp. Are you going to come for me, Makenna?"

The truth was, in this moment she was his, incapable of resisting. She was so far gone, she would do anything he asked.

"Is this what you want? An orgasm at my hand?"

"Yes."

As he moved inside her faster and faster, she dug her toes into the stone floor, lifting herself higher, begging for him to take even more.

"This is the reaction I hoped for. *This* is what I wanted."

Her breaths were too shallow and too fast for her to respond. Masterfully he slid a third finger inside her, then changed the angle of penetration to find her G-spot.

She went rigid as a breath strangled her and she came, whimpering through her screams. Even though she was in the throes of an ecstasy she'd never experienced before, he continued to finger-fuck her. *"Oh my God."*

"Ride it."

Beneath his skillful ministrations, she shattered, losing track of time and space.

When she returned to full consciousness, she was in his lap, cradled in his arms, comforted by his strength and the reassuring thud of his heartbeat. His scent, that of the desert after a stunning electrical storm, filled her senses.

Blinking, she placed a hand on his chest and pushed away from him. "I apologize." Her memory had a gap in it. One moment she was writhing, the next, it was over, and now she was in his arms. "I'm not sure what happened there."

"You gave yourself to me completely." He captured her

chin so that she had to look at him, see the sincerity in his eyes. "And that makes it as spectacular for me as it was for you." His lips twitched in a half smile. "At least I hope you enjoyed it?"

"It was..." Where was her ability to put words to emotion? "Everything I could have hoped for, maybe more. Better than my fantasies." *Did I really admit that?*

"It's completely about you. You came to this with honesty and curiosity, and I merely facilitated the experience."

"I think perhaps you are underestimating your contribution, Sir."

"And you're having a difficult time accepting my compliment," he countered.

Shocking her, he brushed a gentle kiss across her lips. The world around her tilted. What was happening here?

Makenna warned herself not to read anything into his action. His actions—and every word he uttered—had been constructed to make her feel like one in a million. No wonder he had an entire line of women at the ready. She, however, was too smart to become one of them.

"Have you had enough? Or would you potentially like to try out a flogger and the Saint Andrew's cross?"

Again, her survival instinct screamed at her to run while she had the opportunity. Yet the spell he wrapped around her made her want this evening to last forever. And this was her one and only opportunity to scene with him. "I'm curious." Who was this wild, new person inside her?

His smile was the greatest reward.

"Your choice—I can secure you in place, or you can simply hold on."

Being with him had taught her the power of letting go. Interestingly, being in bondage would also allow her that freedom.

"What will it be? Would you like to wear my cuffs?"

His cuffs.

"Makenna?"

"Yes, Sir. I'd like to wear your cuffs."

He helped her to stand, then caught her around the waist when she wobbled.

A moment later, the world righted itself. "Thank you."

"If you're unsteady, then I'm doing my job well." Even in the dim light, his eyes twinkled with masculine deviltry.

"Your ego again, Sir?"

In pure alpha style, he countered her. "Is it ego if it's true?"

With a shake of her head, she grinned.

"When you're ready, walk to the cross and face it."

A moment later, he released his hold on her.

As she drew closer, the structure loomed a little larger than it had from a distance, a little more intimidating. Then, remembering his coaching, she took a couple of deep breaths to settle herself.

Each of his movements echoed off the stone surroundings, and she glanced over her shoulder to see what he was doing. Confoundingly his back was to her, blocking his movements.

When he turned, he held two pieces of leather. Unable to look away, she followed each of his steps as he closed the distance, then walked to the other side of the cross.

She had to tip back her chin to see his face. While he was still the implacable Dominant, the tenderness in his eyes stole her breath.

"Now raise your arms, please."

Within seconds, she was cuffed and secured in place.

"Not that I think you'd ever flee, but I enjoy having you in bondage—your body available to me." He severed their gazes. "And you can't escape as I do this." He captured her breasts, pressing their heavy weight together.

Her breaths were coming in frantic little bursts.

"Do you like this, being at my mercy?"

This was different than the spanking he had just given her. He was more ruthless now, and this new side of him was scarier, but just as compelling—or maybe even more so.

"Do you?"

Instinctively she pulled back, only to discover that she couldn't move more than a couple of inches.

"I noticed the way you whimpered when Alcott squeezed his wife's breasts while he was wearing the vampire gloves."

"That was terrifying."

"But tantalizing, yes?"

She pressed her lips together, unable to give him the confession he wanted.

Relentlessly he pressed his fingernails into her flesh, then captured her nipples, pinching them between his thumbs and forefingers.

She sighed as a fresh wave of need made her weak.

"You like it. Is your pussy getting wet again?"

Impossibly it was. She'd never had multiple orgasms. And the fact that she was already turned on again stunned her.

"I'm going to remove your skirt so that it doesn't impede my swing." He walked around her to tug the material over her hips, then down her legs, leaving her completely exposed and vulnerable to him.

He placed a gentle kiss to her shoulder before leaving her once more.

When he returned, he stood in front of her and held up a short emerald-green suede flogger. "This one is more thuddy than stingy. A perfect choice for your first experience…or as a warm-up."

She gulped.

"Feel free to use your safe word, and I'll slow down at any point. Understand?"

"Yes, Sir." At least she thought so. How could she truly know what to expect?

"We will start slow, and I'll check in with you."

Master Zachary walked behind her and allowed the strands to fall on her buttocks in such a gentle manner that she barely registered the impact.

For minutes, he explored her entire body in that same way, dancing the leather across her skin. Because he was such an expert, she relaxed. Only then did he increase his tempo.

"Are you doing okay?"

"More green than I could have imagined." The leather licked her in bites and whispers, and it was the most exotic, erotic thing she had ever experienced.

Her temporary Dominant flogged her in earnest, and each crisscrossed strike made her wetter and wetter.

Then he stopped and slid a finger between her legs, rubbing so vigorously that her breath caught. *"Fuck.* I think I'm going to come."

"You absolutely will. But not quite yet." He moved his hand away.

In frustration, she stamped her foot.

Instead of showing sympathy, he chuckled. "I would have never guessed you were a brat."

"You, Sir, are a tease."

"There's plenty more where that came from." He fisted a hand in her hair and pulled back her head as he pressed his body against hers, trapping her between his strength—and his dizzying erection—and the unyielding wooden structure. Then he ferociously plundered her mouth, seeking and demanding her surrender.

Helplessly she gave him everything he asked for. He'd made her pussy wet and her nipples hard. She was on fire from his mouth.

Eventually he ended the kiss, leaving her changed. Because of his physical reaction to her, she now had a confidence she'd never before experienced.

After taking a step back, he resumed the flogging, this time harder than before.

Jesus. How was it possible that this was no longer enough? "I...I need more."

"That's my perfect innocent." He flogged her in earnest before dropping the implement to the floor with a loud clatter.

Master Zachary masturbated her, filling her channel with his fingers, going knuckles- deep with long, demanding strokes. "Now, *now* you've earned the orgasm. Give it to me."

She whimpered, arching her back to thrust herself toward him.

He dug his fingers from his free hand into her ass cheek, creating a starburst of pain that rocketed her over the edge. She screamed out his name and climaxed hard, not just once, but twice. And still he wouldn't give up.

"Keep going."

"I can't!" There was nothing left in her, and she wouldn't have remained upright if he hadn't affixed her to the cross.

"You can. I'm hand-fucking you, and I want your orgasm. And you're going to be a good submissive and give it to me. Aren't you?"

He gave her no choice. He took what he demanded, wringing it from her body.

Makenna had no idea how long it went on, but all of a sudden, even in the warm Nevada desert, she was completely chilled.

"Let's get you out of those bonds." He reached around her and pressed his wet fingers to her mouth. "Now lick."

Unable to find her voice, she complied. The eroticism of the act shocked and thrilled her.

Efficiently he detached her from the cross, then rubbed her arms as she slowly lowered them.

Hands on her shoulders, he turned her to face him. "You're shivering." He removed his shirt and draped it over her shoulders, then swept her up and carried her to the bench so swiftly she didn't have time to protest that she was too heavy for him.

And the truth was, he held her as gently as if she were made from spun glass.

She settled against his already familiar body.

What an odd dynamic BDSM was. Some of his spanks had been hard enough to make her yelp. Yet she drew comfort from the same hands that had tortured her. It was a euphoric marriage of pain and pleasure. No wonder so many people were completely addicted to it.

Even though they hadn't had sex, she'd never been closer to anyone—or more vulnerable to emotional hurt.

"How are you doing?"

To mask her real answer, she reached for something that would unravel her tension. "I take back what I said earlier."

"Oh?"

"You're not egotistical."

He responded in kind. "I've ruined you for other men, then?" With the pad of his thumb that still smelled of sex, he traced her lower lip. "It's been a memorable evening for me as well. I'm honored to be the first man you've played with in this way."

First man—which meant he fully expected her to move on to another. Which she'd known all along. So why did his statement sting? "Thanks for a great introduction." She slid from his lap. "And for taking such good care of my things." She'd expected to find her skirt on the ground. But it was neatly stacked along with everything else.

"Let me take off your cuffs."

Grateful for the shirt that gave her some cover, she extended her wrists toward him.

While she dressed, he sanitized the Saint Andrew's cross and repacked his bag. Then she offered him his shirt back.

While he slipped it on, she feasted her gaze on his breathtaking body—the flat, honed planes of his abdomen, the raw strength of his broad shoulders, and the ripple of his bulging biceps.

Though she'd fantasized about him plenty, he blew away every single expectation. More than ever, he'd be the star of her dreams.

He tucked his shirt into his trousers; then, instead of refastening his cuffs, he rolled them up, leaving his forearms exposed. Simply, he was the picture of male perfection.

"Shall we?"

The return to reality was as inevitable as it was unwelcome, leaving her mentally and physically exhausted. "I'm ready to go home."

"I'll see you out."

"That's nice but not necessary. Thank you, though."

"I'm not flexible on this." His jaw was set, and his tone was harsher than anything she'd heard from him. The accommodating Dominant who'd taken her to the dizzying depths of sexual hedonism was gone. In his place was an alpha who would not be dissuaded. "After you, Ms. Helton."

She squared her shoulders in an attempt to gather her composure.

Rather than leading her back through the house, they followed a path that led to the driveway. Once they reached the valet station, she described her car, and the young man nodded and then headed off at a sprint.

"All set. There's no need for you to stay any longer."

"I can only guess what kind of man you're used to being with, but do not confuse me with him."

An eternity later, the valet pulled to a stop in front of them.

Master Zachary handed the man a nice tip. "I've got it from here."

"Yes, sir." With a nod, he moved away to help another guest.

Master Zachary walked Makenna around the car and handed her into the driver's seat. Taking a moment to regain her equilibrium, she fiddled with the air conditioner's controls, even though the setting was fine.

"I'd like to see you again."

Before she could respond, he went on. "May I have your phone number?"

Makenna shook her head. "This was…" She paused. *Magical. Amazing.* "I know you're a busy man, Mr. Denning." She used his surname as a way to distance herself from the temptation. "I had a nice evening."

"Nice?" For a second, he frowned, and his eyes seemed to darken as something flitted through the blue depths. Surely her rejection couldn't have caused him pain.

She reached for the door handle. "I need to be going."

With a tight nod, he stepped back, and she seized the opportunity to seal herself off from him.

As Makenna accelerated, she looked in the rearview mirror and saw him standing where she'd left him, arms folded, legs planted shoulder width apart, looking absolutely fucking furious.

It was then that she realized he'd never returned her panties.

CHAPTER THREE

The driver pulled up behind a long line of limousines and gleaming black vehicles, waiting for his turn to pull under the spectacularly lit pink brick porte cochere.

Because of her job as an event planner, she'd already visited Las Vegas's newest resort and casino several times—once for a soft opening meant to wow—and it still impressed her.

WELCOME TO THE BELLA ROSA was written in massive letters. This afternoon, the gold leaf shimmered in the afternoon sun, offering a mirage-like greeting.

"I'll walk the rest of the way." She paid her bill on the app.

"Fair warning. Give yourself plenty of time when you're ready to leave. It can take forever to get a car out here."

Not a surprise. The billionaire owner, Lorenzo Carrington, had decided not to give the property a theme. Instead, he wanted to offer a high-end luxury experience. From the buzz in the press, it was a good call. Despite its location at the end of the Strip, the property was reported to be packed with customers and thrill seekers who craved elegance. She'd expected that for a period of time after the grand opening, but the number of nights they sold out was on the way to be record-setting. "Thanks for the advice." She handed him a nice cash tip.

"So, give me a call anytime. If I'm available, I'll meet you over there." He pointed to a place separate from the line for taxis and rideshares.

"Thank you." She accepted the business card he offered.

Glad she hadn't opted to wait for a doorman, Makenna walked toward the entrance. The line had barely moved, and guests of all nationalities were buzzing around, laden with designer luggage.

Crisp, cold air engulfed her when she walked through the wide-open entrance. Instantly she was lured by enticing electronic chimes from high-stakes slot machines anxious to separate her from her money.

Numerous nearby tables offered card games and more. Ladies sipped champagne, and men dressed in suits and tuxedos drank whiskey.

A hand-lettered sign indicated the way to the Rose Martini Bar. Every time she visited, she noticed some nuance she'd missed before, from the stunning chandeliers to walls covered with murals that could have been painted by Renaissance masters. The meeting space was stunning as well, and so far away that trams—of course outfitted with opportunities for gaming—shuttled attendees back and forth.

She checked in at the podium and was grateful she had made reservations. Although it was only five o'clock, the place was already standing room only. Makenna wore her work outfit— a royal-blue dress and shoes that matched her purse—and was slightly underdressed for the exclusive lounge. Many places in town were filled with casino-hopping tourists in shorts and flip-flops, but not at the Rose—as the Bella Rosa was already being nicknamed.

"Right this way, Ms. Helton."

She followed the hostess through the space with its signature glass bar pulsing with neon lights. Behind it, three bartenders were pouring and shaking with entertaining flair.

Avery was already seated at a table, studying a leather-bound menu. She slipped from the bar-height stool to give Makenna a hug. "Isn't this place magnificent?"

"Sensational." Makenna had been looking forward to this evening, hoping to get some answers. Since Saturday night, thoughts of Master Zachary had consumed her, and she'd spent far too much time on the internet reading stories about him—including the fact that he was reputed to belong to the Zetas. Known as Titans, the secret society was comprised of the world's richest and most powerful people. World leaders, actors, scientists, writers, and billionaires belonged, along with philanthropists and politicians. Even though no one had confirmed the organization actually existed, plenty speculated that it did.

They both took their seats, and Makenna picked up her menu. A quick glance confirmed that prices started at twenty dollars, even during happy hour. There were at least thirty martini choices—from classic to unique creations.

"I'm sticking with my original idea. I want to try the Italian Wedding Cake. What are you starting with?"

Makenna put down her menu. "Death by Chocolatini."

"I should have guessed!"

The server arrived, and they placed their orders. "May I bring an appetizer?"

They both agreed to wait to order food until Zara arrived.

"All right." Avery leaned forward. "I've been dying of curiosity. How did you end up scening with Master Zachary?"

"It wasn't on purpose." She exhaled. "I was watching the Hewitts in the observation room. And I was so entranced that I didn't notice Master Zachary behind me until he put his hands on my shoulders."

"Dang." Avery shivered deliciously.

"He asked me to describe what was happening." Makenna left out other scandalous details like the fact that he'd asked her to remove her panties. And that he'd spanked her right there in the open. "And then he invited me to the grotto."

"So how was that?"

Complicated. "Everything I could have hoped."

"Are you going to play with him again?"

"No." Makenna knew better than to allow herself to be consumed with a billionaire. But she'd spent the weekend thinking about Master Zachary, even succumbing to temptation and spending Sunday afternoon reading articles about his life.

One socialite had been particularly scathing, saying he wasn't a playboy—he was a manwhore. "You know he never sees the same woman twice." Makenna had scrolled through the pictures that proved it. "Even if he did, I wouldn't be a consideration. I don't have the required social pedigree."

"He's not that shallow."

She wasn't as sure. Men like him wanted a wife who would be an asset, a woman who'd gone to the right schools, had successful parents. With her working-family background, Makenna had nothing in common with him. "I'm not his type, and I don't belong in his world."

"That's what I thought when I met Cole. Being his wife will have some demands, but it's also exhilarating. And I wouldn't have missed this opportunity for the world."

"Despite the stress of the wedding, you seem really happy."

"Honestly? It's beyond my greatest expectations. It meant taking a risk, but it's been worth it."

Her thoughts twirled, and she considered them before speaking. "You're stronger than I am."

"No." Avery placed her hand on Makenna's. "Your asshole ex did a lot of damage, and I hate that he's allowed to impact your future."

She winced. Though Avery was her usual gentle self, her words were barbed, and they stung when they found their target.

"Zachary would be a fool if he didn't want you, and he's a smart man."

"What do you know about him?"

"Not much, except from what I've seen in his interactions with Cole. Zachary is honest, maybe brutally so."

"Maybe. I guess I don't want to be someone he fucks and forgets."

"As if that would happen." She rolled her eyes. "Look, Kenna. Think about giving him a chance. He'll be straight with you about what he wants. At least hear him out?"

And risk my heart?

"You can't stay single your entire life."

"Well…"

They both laughed.

"What if you thought of him as a bridge back into the dating world? He would treat you like a princess."

No doubt that was true.

"You deserve to be wined and dined." Avery's eyes twinkled. "And spanked."

Makenna gasped.

"Go have fun. Don't expect it to be forever. Enjoy his company and a few orgasms."

The drinks arrived in glasses with Z-shaped stems, interrupting conversation.

Avery took a sip of hers. She closed her eyes in bliss. "Oh

my God. It's decadent." She put down her glass. "Now try yours."

Makenna licked some of the sugar and cocoa from the rim, then took a tiny sip. Her taste buds exploded, dancing from the combination of sweet and bitter chocolate, complemented by top-shelf vodka. "Amazing. It's as rich as the man I hope to marry one day."

Giggling at the absurdity since they had both achieved business success and were more than capable of taking care of themselves, they clinked their glasses together.

"And now..." Makenna put down her beverage. "We absolutely have to talk about your wedding plans before we finish this; otherwise I'll never remember anything." She pulled her tablet from her purse and called up Avery's file. "We need to finalize the cocktail hour menu. Are we adding your martini to the list?"

"Absolutely."

Makenna made some changes to the menu, then showed the future bride the new estimated bar tab.

"That'll work."

"How are the RSVPs coming?"

"We already have thirty more people attending than we had planned on."

Makenna nodded. "Would you like to increase the budget, or would you like to make changes to the menu for a less expensive entrée?"

"As I'm sure you've already guessed, Cole is completely against changing the menu."

"Okay then. An increase in budget it is. I'll send you an updated amount tomorrow."

Avery nodded. "And one other thing. Cole would like to have an ice sculpture."

For a wedding, it wasn't a common request, but it was certainly doable. "What did you have in mind?"

"An owl." Avery picked up her cell phone, tapped it a few times. "Let me send you a picture."

When it appeared on Makenna's tablet, she cocked her head to the side. "Athena's owl."

Without answering, Avery took another sip.

"I did a little research." *Hours of it. Days of it.*

"And?"

"Admit it. He's a Titan?"

"I can neither confirm nor deny the allegation."

It wasn't like Avery to hedge. "Saturday when they shook hands, he and Cole were both wearing rings with owls on them. The same one you just sent me."

"I can neither—"

"Confirm nor deny the allegation." Makenna sighed. "You're not going to tell me anything more?"

Zara arrived, forcing them to abandon the conversation. Several men had turned their heads to track her movements. A short formfitting dress hugged her curves. She wore sky-high strappy sandals and had accessorized like crazy with jewelry and a tiny silver clutch. Her hair, brunette burnished with blonde and copper highlights and lowlights, swung at her waist. She owned a marketing company, and she was recognized as a social media influencer, which meant she was her greatest asset.

Makenna admired her friend. She was the youngest of five children. And whereas she could have been the spoiled child of a multimillionaire, she'd stayed away from the family business and instead worked her ass off to make it on her own.

Zara gave each of them a quick hug and kiss on the cheek before sliding into her own chair, adjusting her hem so it didn't reveal more than she wanted to.

The server joined them. "Nice to see you again, Ms. Davis."

"Thanks, Julio." Her smile was as genuine as her delight. "Good to see you."

"The usual?"

She nodded. "Thank you."

"Another round for you ladies?"

"You're a regular," Makenna surmised when they were alone again.

"It's a great place to be seen." She grinned.

"So what's your usual?"

"Rose martini, of course."

Avery scowled. "I read the menu twice. How did I miss it?"

"I'll let you have a taste. Are we ordering food?"

"Any recommendations?"

"Everything is to die for. I think we should get them all and share them."

Avery and Makenna looked at each other and shrugged. "Since Avery and I discussed the wedding, this is a business expense for me."

"And this is one of my last nights out before I'm a married woman. That means I'm in."

Makenna finished her drink, only to find a partially melted piece of Godiva chocolate stuck to the bottom.

Zara provided the first suggestion. "Use your tongue."

Makenna laughed.

"How about a knife or fork?" Avery handed her a wrapped set of silverware.

The confection was gooey and alcohol-soaked, and she held it on her tongue while it dissolved. "I could die happy."

Two stunningly gorgeous men were walking through the bar area. Each stood well over six feet tall, and they were as broad as they were fit. Their dark hair was cut in military precision. Even in a room full of expensive suits, theirs were a notch above. And they were wearing sunglasses.

"Security." Avery lifted her eyebrows.

Since Cole was in that line of business, no doubt she knew what she was talking about.

Zara grinned. "Makes me want to do something naughty."

"And get spanked for it?" Avery laughed.

Shocking Makenna, the men paused at their table. "Ladies."

Zara crossed her legs and sat up a little taller. Did she know them?

This close, the pair bore a striking resemblance. Twins? Brothers? Cousins? And each wore a black tie with a pink rose embroidered on it.

"Ms. Davis." After nodding in Zara's direction, they continued on.

"Something you want to tell us?" Avery demanded.

"No." Her smile was saintly.

The server returned with Zara's drink. The martini was a pale pink, and a rose petal floated on top.

Avery looked at the server. "I'll have one of those.

"For you, ma'am?" He addressed Makenna.

"Lemon drop." Something not quite as sweet as what she'd just finished.

"Any appetizers?"

Zara nodded. "All of them."

"Of course." He closed his order pad and slid it into his apron.

Before her brain became any cloudier, Makenna looked at Avery. "I've been meaning to ask, are we having a bachelorette party?"

Avery nodded. "But not like everyone else does. I was thinking we could do a spa day at the Royal Sterling. I was planning to invite a couple of other friends and maybe some people from the businesswomen's group."

"That would be a strategic move." Makenna nodded. "We can make an afternoon of it and rent out the whole place."

After they all checked their calendars and agreed on suggestions, Makenna made a note to call the spa.

"I'll provide champagne and snacks." Zara shrugged when Avery started to object. "Part of your wedding present."

"That's far too generous."

"Not at all. It's my way of ensuring you'll throw a bachelorette party for me if I ever find a man."

Their drinks and food arrived, and Avery entertained them with gossip about who her eighty-year-old great-aunt Scarlet was dating this week. The Brit was an actor less than half her age and, in her words, a bit too old for her tastes. The burlesque phenomenon was considering dumping him for a recently divorced prince who was still in his thirties.

Avery swirled her drink. "She thinks maybe he can keep up with her. She's tired of waiting for the Brit's little blue pill to make his dick hard."

Makenna laughed so hard that people at the next table turned to face them.

The server paused to ask if they wanted another round.

"I wish I could." Avery sighed. "But I have an early morning."

"I'm attending an open house for a real estate agent. So I have to get going." Zara reached for her purse. "Can we get the check, please?"

"Separate checks?"

"Just one," Makenna replied before anyone else could. "And bring it to me, please."

"I'll get it right out." The server headed back toward the computer.

"Kenna, you don't need to do that." Avery was always the first to protest.

"As I said, it's a business expense."

"In that case, I'll treat next time. We need to do it soon so we're not too far out of balance."

"It's a deal." In that moment, awareness, hot and irresistible, tingled at the base of her spine. Sensing she was being watched, Makenna turned, and her heart slammed into her throat.

Master Zachary stood with a small group of men around a table, and he was looking at her.

Breathless, she returned her attention back to her friends, pretending an earthquake hadn't rocked her world.

"Ah…" Avery glanced over at the other table. "He's headed this way."

Makenna traced the stem of her glass. "I'm sure he's not."

Zara glanced too. "Are you talking about Zachary Denning? Oh! You saw him at the party on Saturday night?"

"Yes." Her thoughts were in pieces.

"Did you play?"

Makenna cleared her throat. "We did."

"And he wants you."

"Definitely not." Makenna dug her credit card from her wallet. Anything to distract herself.

"I can tell you this—he's a man on a mission. But he has to work hard to deserve you. Don't forget that."

Though Makenna tried to steel herself, the effort failed. She was too besotted with the billionaire to pretend otherwise.

"Five seconds," Avery warned. Then she smiled. "Zachary!"

He hugged Avery, then lasered his focus on Makenna. "Ms. Helton." He captured her hand and raised it to his lips, crashing memories through her, reigniting awareness.

"Mr. Denning."

With a knowing, terrifying smile, he released her.

"I know one of your brothers, but we've never been introduced." He turned to Zara. "Zachary Denning."

As was custom, he didn't let on that he recognized her from the scene.

"Zara Davis." The pair shook hands.

"Nice to meet you." But rather than continue the conversation, he returned his attention to Makenna, with the same intensity as he'd shown on Saturday night. "I was hoping to see you again."

Never had she'd been more grateful to be leaving.

The server approached with the check, and Zachary extended his hand. "I'll take that."

"It's mine."

Without argument, Zachary plucked the folio from the server and inserted his black credit card inside without even glancing at the tab.

"You don't need to do that."

"I already did." He returned it to the server.

In true traitorous form, her friends abandoned her.

"Look, Mr. Denning..." She sighed when he slipped into Zara's empty chair. "I don't want to be beholden to you."

"As I said the last time we were together, I don't know what kind of men you've been with, but don't confuse me with them."

"Why are you doing this?"

"I should think it's obvious. Or am I losing my touch?"

"We had a scene. It's over."

"Do you know you look away and blush when you lie?"

She brought her head up sharply. "I'm not—"

"You haven't thought about me? Not even once?"

Did he know the truth? That he'd seeped into her dreams, as well as every waking moment? He was a constant distraction, and she had no idea how to get him out of her mind.

The server dropped off the folio and thanked them.

She couldn't resist a glance as Zachary totaled the bill. The tip he added was exorbitant. Despite herself, she was impressed. As her past taught her, waiting tables was a grueling, difficult job. Customers like him were as rare as they were welcome.

"Have dinner with me."

Makenna blinked. "What?"

"We're already here, and I have reservations at the steak house. My colleague canceled, leaving me at loose ends."

"Thank you, but I have an early morning."

"Another lie."

Her mouth had watered at his suggestion. But the only thing stronger than temptation was the sense of self-preservation. Despite what Avery had suggested, Makenna knew this man would never be a bridge back to the dating world. She was convinced that what he'd said the first night was pure truth. He would ruin her for any other man. And that was a risk she couldn't take.

"I might think you're a little bit of a coward. Ms. Helton."

"Okay, Mr. Denning. You want the truth?" With bravery she didn't really feel, she met his gaze. "You're right, about many things, but not all. I don't have an early morning, and yes, I have been thinking of you. It was a hot scene, so that's natural. Am I a coward? I guess that's for you to decide. I think it's smart, more than anything." She took a breath before she continued. "Will I have dinner with you? Also no. I know your reputation. You want me because you can't have me." Paradoxically, if she gave in to him, he would no longer want her. The trouble was, she'd be left broken. "My answer is no. It will always be no. Keep it up, and I'll tell you to fuck off."

"Fair enough."

She narrowed her eyes. Relenting didn't seem to be something he was familiar with.

"At least let me drive you home."

"I was planning to catch a ride share."

"In that case, I'll walk you out."

Knowing she couldn't win every argument, she gathered her belongings. He stood instantly and offered a hand when she slid off the chair.

As she now expected, he showed a possessive streak by placing his fingertips in the small of her back as they walked to the exit.

She sighed when she saw the line for rides, remembering too late that she should have called her driver. Though they stood under a small shelter, the sun was still brutal, shimmering off the pavement. A tiny drop of perspiration traced down her spine.

"Any other objections to me taking you home?"

She sighed.

"You can say thank you at any time." He strode to the valet stand and handed off his ticket. Before the line had moved at all, his car was brought around.

He dismissed the valet and opened her door, handing her into the luxurious passenger compartment of his low-slung and ultra-expensive sports car.

"Thank you."

"That's better."

Within moments, they were on the road. Following her directions, he threaded his way through the city to her townhome in Henderson.

"Nice place." He slid the gear shifter into Park.

She looked at the stucco structure that shared walls with three other units. At least hers had some flowers on the tiny front porch. "It's not what you're used to."

"You make a lot of assumptions."

"Do I?" She faced him. "You're not a billionaire? A Titan?"

"You've been busy."

"A manwhore?"

"A—" He blinked, and then he laughed. "That's a new one."

She hadn't expected that reaction.

"To respond the same way you did... Do I date? Yes. A lot?" He shrugged. "I guess that depends on your definition. Do I use women?" Something dangerous pulsed in his temple. "Hell no." He bumped down the temperature in the car. "I don't care what opinions of me are out there. The only thing I care about is what you think."

"You're good." She scoffed. "I'll grant you that. Almost good enough to make me believe you mean it."

"Good night, Makenna." That ticking became more pronounced. The way he said it was his version of *fuck you.*

He pressed the button to kill the engine. "I'll walk you to the door." Motions deliberate, he exited the vehicle and waited for her to do the same. Then he followed her up the path.

Once she inserted the key in the lock, he turned and strode back to the car.

Her hand shook. What had she done?

You saved yourself.

So why didn't she believe that?

The engine kicked back on, and she went inside, closing the door and collapsing against it.

Tires squealed, and then she was left with nothing but the loud and horrible deafening sound of silence.

∽

Zachary strode across the red carpet to reach the back of Bella Rosa's whiskey and cigar bar where Cole was already seated.

This was one space where the owner had exercised his

personal preferences and designed it based on his interpretation of an old-world gentlemen's club with oversize leather chairs arranged around small tables. Walls and partitions were decorated with black-and-white pictures of old Las Vegas, including signed pictures of the era's best-known entertainers. The lounge boasted Sin City's best bartenders, a walk-in humidor, and a dizzying number of whiskeys.

Seating was limited, and admission was for members only, making it a perfect place for deal-making and clandestine meetings.

Cole stood, and the two shook hands.

After Zachary took his chair, he leaned forward. "Do you have the file?" On Sunday morning, after his team hadn't turned up the information he hoped to find on Makenna Helton, he'd contacted Cole. If she was hiding any secrets, he would find them.

"I do." He extracted a thumb drive from a pocket inside his sports coat. Instead of turning the device over, he placed it on the table directly in front of him.

"Problem?"

"You tell me."

Zachary sat back. "I wouldn't have hired you if it wasn't important."

"Why the interest in Makenna?"

"It's personal."

Cole, too, sat back, and he steepled his hands.

Before Zachary could guess what fucking game Cole was playing, the server arrived bearing a tray that contained a sealed bottle of whiskey and two glasses.

"I'll take it from here." Cole gave the woman a quick smile of dismissal. "Thank you."

Zachary had readily agreed to meet Cole here. The ambience of the whiskey and cigar bar was second to none, and it had quickly become one of the best places to meet up with other Titans. He'd been one of the first people to buy a condominium in the residence tower, and the fact that he had access to several private elevators allowed him to move around the resort without being seen. "Nice bottle."

"Ridiculously expensive. Julien Bonds sent me a bottle recently."

"Nice."

Bonds was a quirky fellow, tech billionaire and dreamer, with his fingers in every pie.

"I liked that shit so much that I ordered a case. The bar manager ordered a few bottles for my private reserve."

Not only did Lorenzo have a whiskey sommelier on duty, but he'd also installed private liquor cabinets. For a ludicrous annual fee, members could rent one of the glass lockers. The member's name was inscribed on a brass plaque and affixed to the wood beneath.

Of course, no one could bring in a bottle. It had to be ordered through the hotel's preferred distributor, and the price was marked up considerably.

Cole broke the seal. "Bastard knows what he's doing. Gives away one bottle and gets an order for twelve more."

Zachary nodded. "Brilliant."

"Fucking genius," Cole corrected, pouring a couple fingers' worth of the premium whiskey in the cut crystal glasses.

By unspoken assent neither of them returned to business until after they had completed their first whiskey.

Then, after Cole had refreshed their drinks, he leaned back. "Makenna is one of my future wife's best friends."

Zachary nodded.

"Avery will kill me if I have any part in hurting her."

"I assure you that is not my intent."

In silence, Cole regarded his friend. "Then what is?"

"Being sure."

Cole scowled. "Of what?"

How the hell did he explain something even he didn't understand? The untamed passionate response he'd had for a woman he barely knew.

He was willing to admit he loved scening with newbies. Coaxing their reactions, teaching them about their own bodies' pleasure receptors was intoxicating.

And yet... Makenna was different. She was more real than any other submissive he'd been with. They'd had a connection he hadn't known possible.

He'd envied Cole when he found Avery, but Zachary hadn't understood how any man would willingly throw away the perks of bachelorhood and get involved in wedding preparations.

Now? *Yeah.* He got it. He more than wanted Makenna—he burned for her, and it was fucking consuming him. Sleep was impossible, and far too many business details had slipped.

And yet... Was he blinded by his own lust? Making a second mistake? "There was a woman."

While Zachary struggled, Cole waited.

"During my stint in the military, I avoided relationships. That changed when I came home. My mother set me up with a woman of impeccable background. I was prepared to refuse to take her on a date, but Blythe was beautiful, and I was smitten. She played hard to get. The more she turned me down, the more I chased her. I was in love. Or I thought I was." He picked up his glass and rolled it between his palms. No one had ever heard this story. "It took forever to get her in my bed, and even longer to get her to accept my marriage proposal."

"I'm listening."

The memory still burned. A few months before their wedding, he'd arrived home from work to find her in the bathtub. He was surprised to hear a man's voice. Quietly Zachary opened the door to discover she was videoing herself while she masturbated. And the words he heard seared into his memory.

"What do you want?" the male on the screen had demanded.

"Your big dick. I need you to fuck me so I can forget my miserable life. The asshole made me sign a prenup. If we get divorced in the first five years, I don't get anything for putting up with his shit."

Fury seared Zachary.

"How long until you can see me? I gotta fill that hot cunt of yours."

"Next week. I'm on one of his credit cards, and I told him I have a girls' weekend."

He'd heard enough.

With icy calm, he crossed the room and plucked the phone from her hand.

"Zach! I can explain. It's not what you think."

He turned and slammed the screen on the sharp edge of the quartz counter; then he tossed the device into the bathtub with her.

By then, she was standing, and bubbles clung to her body in invitation. With a smile, he took her hand.

"Zach?" Her eyes were wide, and her breaths were short, frightened.

As she watched, he slid his grandmother's ring off Blythe's finger. He turned, walked away, and never spoke another word to her.

He shook his head, realizing Cole was still waiting. "I got played. It could have cost me big—nearly did. She was in love with someone else, and they intended to be together, using my money. I was a fool, and I'm fucking embarrassed to admit it. To say I don't trust people easily is accurate."

Cole nodded, and he leaned forward to slide the thumb drive in front of Zachary. Continuing to roll his glass, he stared at the small USB that would expose every one of Makenna's shortcomings. Once he opened the dossier, she'd have no secrets from him.

After a moment's hesitation, he picked up the drive and dropped it into his pocket.

Because part of him hated what he'd done, he finished the rest of the whiskey in a single swallow.

For the next few minutes, they continued to talk, and his tension eased; then he followed Cole's gaze toward the other side of the room and saw the casino owner walking toward them.

Zachary and Cole stood to shake Lorenzo Carrington's hand. As always, he was impeccably dressed in only the finest bespoke garments from Italy. Though his mother had tried to distance herself from her family, blood ran deep, and Lorenzo had fully embraced her side of the family. Don Marco La Rosa himself was reputed to be an investor in the property.

Cole would know for sure, and Zachary wouldn't be surprised to learn that the rumor was true. After all, not a lot of people had the resources to invest billions of dollars in a brand-new resort.

"Join us?" Cole invited. "It's the Bonds whiskey."

Lorenzo raised an eyebrow. "I believe I will." He signaled to the two men who were with him. One took his place several feet behind Lorenzo, while the other positioned himself at the back of the room, where he could watch all the comings and goings.

Instantly, the server appeared with another glass. This one contained a hand-carved ice ball.

Cole poured while speaking. "Avery tells me we haven't gotten your RSVP for the wedding."

"I'll be there." He inclined his head toward his bodyguards. "Plus two. They will not require meals."

The billionaire no doubt garnered significant interest from the female population, but he never dated as far as Zachary knew.

Lorenzo took a sip of the whiskey. "Excellent. Perhaps we'll consider stocking it."

"If you do, tell Bonds I want a commission."

He placed his almost untouched glass back on the table. "I'll allow you to handle those details."

Lorenzo's man moved closer to him. With a brief nod, Lorenzo stood. "If you'll excuse me, duty calls."

With that, he exited through an unseen door next to a perhaps unironic picture of Bugsy Siegel, a legendary Las Vegas mobster.

"Speaking of RSVPs…" Cole finished his drink. "I guess you can't invite Makenna as your guest because she's the wedding planner."

"Asshole."

"Between you and Lorenzo, I'll tell Avery we need a table for the Lonely Hearts Club."

"Don't rub it in, man."

Cole grinned.

"Thanks for the report."

They both stood and shook hands. "Don't make me regret it."

Cole's words stayed with him long into the night. Around midnight, he inserted the USB into his computer.

But instead of opening the file, he typed in a command to reformat the drive, erasing all the data.

CHAPTER FOUR

"You are absolutely radiant!" Makenna exclaimed. She'd been with her friend when she found her gown, but now—waiting to walk down the aisle—Avery looked like a fairy princess.

They exchanged air hugs so that the makeup artist's work wasn't ruined. "Are you ready?"

"Emotionally?" Avery exhaled. "Yes. But nervous about all the details."

"That's why I'm here. Most of the guests have arrived." Including more VIPs than she'd ever dealt with, from Lorenzo Carrington to a reclusive associate of Cole's known only as Hawkeye—Makenna had no idea if that was a first or last name. "The minister is on-site. And I have to say, the ballroom is even more beautiful than our renderings. I'm sure you'll be pleased."

The event space had been transformed with pipe and draping, balloon arches, several beautiful spots for pictures, massive flower arrangements on pedestals, and multiple bars had been set up strategically to minimize waiting.

The ballroom opened onto a patio. Tables were arranged

in conversational style, and bright-purple umbrellas added a festive flair. And of course, a bar had been set up outside as well.

"Has Cole arrived yet?"

Makenna grinned. "He's been at the hotel since noon."

Avery opened her eyes wide. "Are you serious?"

"He's been greeting people and pestering me. He wants to see you."

"What? No." She shook her head vehemently. "I haven't kept this gown secret for months for him to ruin the surprise."

"That's what I thought, but I promised I'd relay the message."

After glancing around to be sure no one was in earshot, Avery leaned close to Makenna. "You can only guess what his favorite form of stress release is."

Makenna pressed her lips together so she didn't laugh out loud. "I'm not sure that would be good for your dress or your hair."

"Not to mention my rear end. And it's been tormented enough."

"Okay, okay." Makenna laughed. "I'll make sure he doesn't get within ten feet of you. He's afraid you'll change your mind."

"The man is impossible when he wants something."

"He's in love."

"Yeah." Avery's expression softened. "So am I."

Makenna checked her watch. "Less than half an hour. I want to do a final check. I'll be back in about fifteen minutes."

There was a knock on the suite's door.

"Want me to get it?" Zara was serving as one of Avery's bridesmaids, and she was the only one who'd finished getting ready.

"Thanks." Avery nodded. "But if it's Cole, don't let him in."

Moments later, Avery's great-aunt Scarlet swept in wearing a long sequined gown and an ornate fascinator hat. No doubt her picture would be on social media before the ceremony began.

Scarlet smiled at everyone before homing in on Avery. "Darling girl! You are positively sensational!"

Makenna left, not that anyone noticed.

Once she was in the service elevator, she glanced at her tablet and was relieved not to see any messages. Things seemed to be under control.

Downstairs, she surveyed the anteroom where the cocktail hour would be hosted. Bar-height tables were scattered around and festively decorated with the wedding colors. Servers were prepping trays for champagne and hors d'oeuvres.

Then, for one last time, she walked through the ballroom where the reception would be held. Everything was complete, and the band was setting up.

Satisfied, she continued through to the patio. Zachary was there, elbow propped on top of a metal fence. He was devastating in a charcoal-colored suit. His tie was perfectly in place. Despite the heat, he was cool and composed.

Even though it had been over a month since she had seen him, he took her breath away. Time and distance had done nothing to quell her desire for him. In fact, it had made it worse.

At night when she was lonely, she wondered what her life might have been like if she had agreed to dinner or another scene.

He looked her up and down, slowly, measuredly taking in every detail.

Though she should make polite conversation and then

leave, she remained where she was, not wanting the moment to end.

"How am I doing?"

In confusion, she blinked, not following his question. "I'm sorry?"

"At fucking off?"

Makenna winced. Then, to hide her reaction, she clutched her tablet closer to her chest.

"Since you're such a detective, how many dates have I been on in the past month?"

"I have no idea." She refused to admit that she searched his name nearly every morning when she arrived at her office.

"Either you're catching a sunburn, or you're lying again."

Damn you.

"None. And you know it." He pushed away from the fence and devoured the distance between them. "I was in love once."

With his fiancée, Blythe, no doubt. Makenna had read a couple of articles about the short-lived engagement. Shortly thereafter, his office had issued a short statement, saying he wished her well while asking that their privacy be respected.

Unsure where his comment was headed, Makenna waited. She had a lot to do, but she didn't want to dismiss him right away.

"Blythe was in love too. With another man." His words were flat, but no doubt pain lingered behind them.

"I'm sorry."

"Don't be. I'm glad I found out when I did. She and her lover concocted a scheme to make me fall for her. Scary thing was how close it came to working."

"Meaning you sleep with a different woman every week because you have trust issues?" This close, he overwhelmed her. He smelled of spice, and his body language spoke of determination.

Instead of responding to her barb, he took a half step toward her. "She knew how long we had to stay married to get the amount of money she wanted." A combination of anger and pain was mixed in his voice.

"Why are you telling me this?"

"You don't have a monopoly on pain, Makenna, or on the need to protect yourself."

The idea of self-assured billionaire Dominant Zachary Denning having an emotional weakness was so stunning she couldn't respond.

"Or the fact that our behavior doesn't always make sense. After Blythe, I wondered why I'd ever want to get married. I have nieces and nephews, charitable organizations I support. There was no reason for me to have my own children. And then I met you."

"I…" Aware of the time ticking, she frowned. "I don't understand."

"You're different." He propped a finger beneath her chin. *"I'm* different with you. And you know it. There comes a time when we have to stop letting our pain define who we are. When you're ready, I'll be here."

With that, he strode off, leaving her standing there staring after him. She wasn't sure how long she looked at the closed door, but she missed a call from her assistant, Riley.

Her heart still thundering, mind spinning with the implications of everything he'd said, Makenna forced herself to refocus as she hit redial on her assistant's number.

Despite a few momentary lapses, she managed to get back to Avery's suite within the promised fifteen minutes. After advising the bride that it was time to go, she took a staff elevator so that she'd be available at the wedding if anything went wrong.

Makenna blinked back her emotion when Cole saw Avery for the first time. The big, tough secret agent man wiped a tear from his cheek.

Despite herself, Makenna sought out Zachary, but he never glanced back at her.

Avery and Cole exchanged vows they'd written themselves, and then the minister pronounced them husband and wife, partners for life. "You may now kiss your bride."

Cole capitalized on the opportunity, to the cheers and applause of their guests.

Zachary's words still heavy on her heart, Makenna dived back into action, helping organize wedding photos while Riley oversaw the cocktail hour, complete with Avery's favorite martini.

Before the ballroom doors were opened, Makenna double-checked to be sure the ice sculpture had been placed.

Then the reception began in earnest.

A few times during the evening, she was aware of Zachary's gaze on her, and she wondered what she was going to do about him.

Follow Avery's advice and take a chance? Or hide and let her past dictate her future?

Near midnight, the band struck up a ballad, and he strolled over to her. "Dance with me?"

"I'm the hired help."

"You're also one of her best friends."

Was there anything she wanted more than to be in his arms?

"You have an assistant who is keeping watch."

His earlier words returned to her. *"I'm different with you. And you know it. When you're ready, I'll be here."* She sighed, foolishly giving in to temptation. "Just one."

"I'll settle for that...but I'll ask for more."

"You're impossible."

A devilish grin transformed his features, making him even more dangerous, and when he extended his hand, she accepted it.

With effortless ease, his steps graceful, he led her around the floor. "Where did you learn to dance?"

"Something all Titans are required to do."

"That's ridiculous." She laughed and relaxed, surrendering to the pleasure of the moment. Being this close with him was natural, and every one of her feminine instincts responded to him.

The song ended, and he released her. "I enjoyed that. Thank you."

"The pleasure was mine." With a small bow, he walked away, and she had to fight off the temptation to call him back and tell him she was ready for the dinner he'd once suggested.

Her phone chimed. Of course she still had details to attend to, including getting Cole to take care of the bill.

Generally at this part of the evening, the person responsible for the final payment made a crack about the cost of everything, but Cole merely scrawled his signature on the bottom line. "A bargain at ten times the cost." He handed her the pen. "Thank you for being such a good friend. I hope I can attend your wedding soon."

"I'm in no hurry. It's enough to see you happy."

"We'll get together for dinner after we return from our honeymoon."

"Let me know if you need help with anything while you travel."

A few minutes later, Avery sought out Makenna. "I'm sorry you didn't get to enjoy yourself."

"Don't worry about me. I had a good time." The dance with Zachary had been the only thing she needed.

"This has been everything I could have hoped for." She

squeezed Makenna's hands in gratitude. "You're the best wedding planner ever. I couldn't have done it without you." Then she caught sight of her husband. "I'm going to treat you to a spa day when I'm back."

Arm in arm, Avery and Cole headed for the elevator, her veil billowing beautifully behind her.

"Another successful evening, boss." Bearing a glass of champagne, Riley joined her.

Makenna accepted the gift. As a rule, she never drank at an event until it was almost over. "Thank you." Tonight, she really appreciated the expensive glass of bubbly. "You can go ahead and leave anytime."

"It's my turn to stay."

"I don't mind." Especially since Zachary was still here. "But I'm going to sleep for two weeks."

"Meaning you'll be at the office at seven on Monday morning?"

She blew out a breath. "About right." Work was the story of her life. But at least she could take off most of tomorrow. And maybe before bed she'd soak in a hot bath to ease some of the stress of being on her feet—and in heels—since noon.

Over the next hour, other guests left, some saying they were heading to other bars, a few to the casino floor. The cleaning crew got to work—sweeping up glitter, boxing the cake, scooping up balloons.

And then she saw him. Zachary. All thought of resistance fled.

He stood near the exit, his tie loose, and his suit coat slung casually over his shoulder. "You look exhausted."

"Such a charmer."

"I was going to offer to buy you a drink, but I see you already have one."

"Unfortunately I can't finish it since I need to go home."

Makenna half expected him to offer to take her, but he surprised her instead.

"We could go to my condo."

"Which is where?"

"The Bella Rosa."

"Are you serious?" She gaped. "You drove me all the way to Henderson last month, even though you live at the Bella Rosa?"

"Spending time with you is no hardship. Well, until you tell me to fuck off."

"I didn't." She recalled the way his tires had burned on the pavement. "Well, not exactly."

"What do you say? A nightcap at the martini bar? Or I can have catering send up a bottle of champagne."

She couldn't believe she was considering his idea.

"I have a soaker tub."

Tempted, she wrinkled her nose. "You were right about me being tired, and I need my Epsom salts."

"Got you covered. Pulled my hamstring a few months ago. My massage therapist recommended I buy a bag. I still have most of it left—eucalyptus and spearmint scented."

"Mr. Denning…"

"Everything is on your terms. If you want to kick off your shoes and have a glass of champagne before you go to sleep, that's all that will happen."

She shouldn't.

"What do you say?"

"You had me at eucalyptus and spearmint."

*

"Your home for as long as you desire, my innocent." He pressed his thumb pad on a touchscreen on the wall, right below a plaque that read PENTHOUSE TWO, and the door snicked open.

"Welcome home, Mr. Denning."

The greeting was disembodied, female, and Australian, if Makenna's guess was right.

"Temperature is sixty-eight degrees. A shipment of whiskey arrived this afternoon, compliments of Julien Bonds, and you have an 8:15 a.m. appointment with the London office. There have been no updates of note to the world money markets. Though your cryptocurrency has made moves in the past hour. You're on track for your new car." Silence hung for a moment as Zachary closed the door behind them. *"Do you have a guest with you?"*

He looked at Makenna. "Cole installed this. It's a version of Bonds's *Hello, Molly*. Everything electronic in the house talks to her—refrigerator, freezer, wine chiller, air conditioner, water heater, all the security devices. She's one hell of a computer."

"Hmph. I beg your pardon?"

"I mean her AI is state of the art. She's not just a computer."

"That's better."

Makenna laughed. "And she has personality."

"You clearly have a guest, Mr. Denning."

"I do."

"May I say it's about time? You've been a member of the Lonely Hearts Club for too long."

He groaned. "Uhm, system glitch. She's not perfect yet."

"Care to tell me more?"

He rolled his eyes. "Cole. The VIP table?"

"With Hawkeye and Lorenzo Carrington and others?"

"He said it was for us loser bachelors. Even wrote that on the invitation. He filled in the RSVP card himself—*plus zero*."

"Ouch." She flashed him a mock wince.

"Yeah. Asshole makes his happiness known every chance he gets."

"Mr. Denning, would you like to introduce me to your company?"

"I would." To Makenna he explained, "She will learn your voice. If you are introduced, it means that she will respond to your commands."

"What happens if you don't do that?"

"Then she won't follow orders. It's a security precaution." He crossed to a thick glass control panel that was at least eight feet tall. It resembled something out of a science fiction movie. After touching it with his thumb, he gave an instruction. "Miss Ellie, I'd like to you to meet Makenna."

"Hello, Makenna."

Zachary nodded to Makenna. "Say anything in response."

This was so tech-forward her mind whirled. "It's nice to meet you, Miss Ellie."

"I await your commands."

"Wow. That's impressive."

"She is when she wants to be, and when my friends aren't messing with her programming." His grimace was more of a snarl. "Miss Ellie, open the blinds."

Makenna expected to be wowed, but nothing happened.

"Fuck me running." He sighed. "Miss Ellie, *please* open the blinds."

Silently they rose.

As he no doubt intended, Makenna was instantly drawn toward the floor-to-ceiling windows. "It's like being on top of the world." Whenever she was on the Strip, she expected to look out and see neon everywhere, but since they were so high up, she looked down on nearby buildings. "It must be spectacular during the day."

"Mountain view. I'm sure it'll take your breath away, if Miss Ellie decides to cooperate."

She grinned. "Do you always have to say please?"

"Only when she's annoyed at me. Bonds said I can be too impatient, so he programmed an etiquette module into this particular system. At times, I consider disabling her."

"I heard that."

"Let me show you around."

Penthouse Two was spectacular. In addition to a kitchen with high-end appliances and finishes, he had a formal dining room and a separate bar area, perfect for entertaining.

He showed her two of the three bedrooms, and one served as his office. Instead of facing a wall, his desk was situated so he could stare out the window.

She wandered over to his credenza, the only spot in the condominium that was in the least bit messy. Here, file folders and papers were stacked haphazardly.

"I wasn't expecting company."

Makenna couldn't resist teasing him. "As a card-carrying member of the Lonely Hearts Club, of course you weren't." That inadvertent piece of information from the posh Miss Ellie soothed Makenna. She picked up a framed picture of him, taken from behind. He stood with his hands propped on his waist, looking outside. The caption read, "Sky's the limit."

She put it down and turned to him.

"One of the reasons I wanted to live in the clouds." He shrugged. "It's a visual reminder every day to keep working my ass off."

"I like it."

"Let me show you to my bedroom."

His suite was enormous, with an informal seating area at the far end, with two barrel chairs—each with a matching ottoman. A small metal table stood between them. He'd angled them so they faced the window. True to his word, an ice bucket stood there, champagne chilling in it. "May I pour you a glass?"

"Thank you."

He uncorked the expensive bottle and filled two flutes. Before their first sip, his phone rang. "I apologize."

"It's late."

"Overseas, it's tomorrow." He checked his watch. "Or, actually, later today since it's almost one o'clock. Make yourself comfortable. I have an extra robe in my closet, and you'll find the jar of Epsom salts on the teak bench near the tub. Good place for your bubbly as well."

While he answered the summons, she found the promised robe. Holding it close, she crossed into the bathroom. The tile and marble exuded the same elegance as a world-class spa.

Within minutes, she sank chin-deep into the hot, fragrant water.

More tired and relaxed than she'd been in a long time, Makenna lifted her hair so it didn't get wet, then rested the back of her head on the attached pillow. With a sigh, she closed her eyes.

The soft rumble of Zachary's baritone reached her, soothing her. She must have drifted off for a moment, because when she opened her eyes, she was chilled.

Sitting up, she drained the tub and stepped onto the bath mat to reach for her robe. The fluffy material swaddled her in luxury. After picking up the still-full flute of bubbles, she returned to the bedroom to find him seated in one of the chairs with his feet propped on an ottoman. He wore a soft black T-shirt and black pants and was peering out the window over his steepled hands.

As she approached, he turned and smiled. "A fantasy come true."

"You flatter me too much."

"Join me?"

She curled up in the chair. "Maybe I should book a night

at a hotel after every event. Relaxing and not driving… I could get used to this."

"Certainly factored in my decision to buy here. I travel frequently, and I keep similar though much-smaller homes in London, New York, Los Angeles. You'd enjoy them."

"My life is here."

"And you do a hell of a job. No wonder you're in high demand."

"You had a good time?"

"I shared a dance with a very special lady." He refreshed his champagne. "Then she accompanied me home. Yeah. I had a good time. And it's just beginning." In silent invitation, he extended his hand toward her.

This—he—was something she wanted more than her next breath.

They both placed their drinks on the small table.

With a confidence unlike her, she went to him. Then, facing him, she lowered herself into his lap, her knees on either side of his legs.

His eyes darkened and then narrowed. "I've thought of this for weeks, months."

"Months?"

"I had my eye on you at the Hewitts' parties, waiting for my opportunity."

How could she be less vulnerable than he was? "I've wanted this also."

"Have you?" He parted the lapels of her robe, then slid the material over her shoulders. "Your breasts are gorgeous. A gift from the gods." He cupped them in his palms, then tightened slightly. "Since we've had a drink, we can't enjoy a formal scene."

"I promise you I'm not tipsy." Maybe a little bit in an altered state from being near him.

"Earlier I said nothing would happen here unless you wanted it. And I meant it."

"You can believe me when I say that I want you to fuck me."

"Hell no. I want to make love to you. I won't allow you to use words that put emotional distance between us."

"Zachary…I just want to enjoy the moment."

"I'll see to it that you do."

She dropped her hands onto his shoulders as he tightened his grip on her breasts. "Ruin me for any other man?"

"I was honest about my intentions from the start." He placed one hand behind her head and drew her to him so that he could kiss her passionately, asking, seeking, demanding, taking.

When he released her, she moaned and leaned heavily against him.

"Fuck, Makenna. You're everything I want. Everything I need." He tormented her nipples until they were hard and throbbing. Then he sucked on one, laving it with his tongue, swirling and twirling, driving her mad.

She ground herself against his already-hard cock.

"Do you have any idea how much I want you?"

"Maybe as much as I want *you?*"

"I have condoms. But they're across the room."

"I'm not on birth control." She bunched his T-shirt in her hands. "What are we going to do?"

"Solve the problem."

Impossibly, with her laughing and protesting, he managed to stand. "Wrap your legs around me."

"I am way too big for you to do this."

He began to walk, and she yelped. "*You'll drop me!*" Quickly she grabbed hold of his shoulders.

"At some point, we're going to have sex in this position."

"You'll definitely need the Epsom salts after that."

"One more self-deprecating comment out of you, and I promise I'll turn you over my knee tomorrow and paddle you so hard you won't sit for a week."

Not doubting his sincerity, she clamped her mouth closed.

"That's better." They reached the nightstand. "This is going to take some teamwork."

"You could put me down."

"Not happening."

"Do you know how ridiculous this is?"

Immediately he countered her objection. "Do you know how much I fantasized about having you ride my dick while I watch our reflection in the window?"

Her mouth dried.

"You're not the only voyeur, Makenna."

"Uhh…"

"I'm going to keep hold of you. And you're going to open the drawer and pull out a condom."

On the second attempt, she managed to do as he asked. But trying to close the drawer again was futile.

"Leave it. We have other things we need to focus on." He strode back to the living room and managed to sit without either of them losing their balance.

"If you'd have asked me, I would have said that was impossible."

He cracked a grin. "Sky's the limit."

"I'm starting to believe you."

"Where were we?"

"You were sucking my nipple, and I was trying to get myself off on your dick. I want you inside me."

"And it will absolutely happen." As he swept his gaze over her, he sucked in a breath. Very deliberately, he pushed her breasts together and traced gentle circles on her nipples.

"This is overwhelming."

"Good. Now open your mouth for me."

When she did, he stuck a finger inside. "Wet it."

Despite the fact they weren't scening, the man was still every inch a Dominant. When he was satisfied, he pulled it out. "Now, kneel up for me." He slid the damp finger between her feminine folds, tantalizing and arousing her. I want you wet for me."

The mere thought of him was enough to make her needy.

"I want to have sex with you a dozen times and in a dozen different ways. So I need to make sure you don't get too sore."

She clamped her mouth shut; arguing with him would get her nowhere. He played with her pussy and her breasts until she tipped her head back, sending her hair cascading over her shoulders.

His touch left her breathless and desperate. "If you keep this up, I'm going to come. But I want to orgasm with you inside me."

"There's no doubt that will happen as well." He inserted a finger inside her, then slipped in a second.

Trying to rub herself on him, Makenna jerked her hips. *"Please."*

"I need you up on your knees again."

Makenna wiggled around, and somehow he managed to lower his pants and kick them aside. Beneath them—thank God—he was commando. Her first sight of his cock made her gasp. "It's enormous." And a drop of precum leaked from the tip.

"Look what you do to me, my innocent. Can you give me a little room?"

She did as he asked, holding on to the curve of the chair for balance while he rolled the condom down his shaft.

"I'm thinking that your dick is the Eighth Wonder of the World."

"Okay, now it's certain. I will never let you go." With primal intent, he caught her mouth once more, plunging in deeply, simulating sex, claiming her in ways no one else ever had.

With a groan, he captured her hips and drew her toward him once again. His constant approval gave her newfound confidence, and she reached between them to hold his cock while she lowered herself onto his shaft.

She took only a small amount of him inside her before she lifted herself away from him. "It's been a really long time for me."

"We can go as slow as you need."

God. Could she even do this? "That was only your cockhead."

"We're going to be the perfect fit."

He squeezed her ass so hard that she pitched forward. Master Zachary definitely knew what he was doing.

"Now ride me." He kneaded her flesh and gave her multiple swats that made her writhe, and each motion took her lower on his dick until he was seated balls-deep.

With a sigh, she rested her forehead on his shoulder.

"What did I tell you? Perfect fit."

"Is that what you call it?" He filled her completely, owned her. Like the scene they'd shared at the grotto, he was focused solely on her pleasure.

The moment seared into her memory. Zachary Denning, with his approval and the way he continually saw to her well-being, had gotten past her well-constructed defenses. Not only did she care for him—he'd earned her trust.

Slowly she began to move, and she grabbed hold of his shirt and tugged it from his waistband.

He took over from there, pulling it up and off, then tossing it aside.

"Damn." His chest was magnificent, and his abs were honed. "You're absolutely beautiful."

He swiveled the chair slightly. "Look at your reflection. Watch yourself. Watch us." With great deliberation, he gently spanked her, reddening her buttocks.

The image of them moving together, the way his jaw was set, the way his muscles flexed from exertion, drove her to the edge.

"Are you getting ready to come, little innocent?"

"Yes. Y*es.*"

He stopped moving his hips, and she changed their angle, taking what she needed. "That's it." He fisted a hand into her hair to pull back her head, then kissed the hollow of her throat.

She had never been so lost before.

Zachary squeezed one of her nipples. Then he gently bit. The pinprick of pain rocketed her over the edge. Whimpering, crying his name, she took her orgasm, riding it for everything she could. And then her body went limp. He was there, cradling her. When she caught her breath, he brushed a lock of hair back over her shoulder.

"Now I have an idea for your second orgasm."

CHAPTER FIVE

Zachary rearranged the furniture and beckoned to his beautiful, hesitant lover. "I want you to grab the far end of the table, facing the window."

She scowled. "This will never work."

He was taller than she was, but not so much that the position was unachievable. "I assure you, it will."

"Maybe the back of the chair would be better?"

Was she stalling, or doing geometry? "Humor me."

With a skeptical sigh, she did as he said. Zachary moved behind her, placed his hands on her hip bones, then brought her back toward him, holding her steady, effectively imprisoning her.

His cock throbbed with demand. And he held himself in check. This had to be wonderful for her. He'd been waiting for weeks. What were a few more minutes? "Spread your legs as far as you can."

Makenna glanced back, and her eyebrows were knitted together over her expressive cornflower-blue eyes.

"There's no doubt I'm going to fill your tight little cunt." She was still wet, and he inserted the tip of his cock into her.

She did a little dance but then faced forward.

In the window's reflection, he watched her long blonde hair fall forward to frame her face.

Her upturned ass was a dream, reminding him of the night she'd lain across his lap at the Hewitts' party. She'd been shivering from anticipation and maybe a touch of fear, but still she'd trusted him.

He admired her. No doubt it had been difficult for her to keep her insecurities in check while he skimmed his fingers across her skin, exploring her innermost secrets, then spanking her until she wore one of his handprints like a badge of glory.

He eased into her, looking at their bodies in the window. Soft and hard, feminine and masculine. "Your breasts are magnificent." They swayed and bounced, making him even harder.

Zachary shook his head to clear it. If he wanted to last more than thirty seconds, he needed to change things up.

He pulled out slightly, then took a breath. Control regained, he slid his forearm in front of her, so she couldn't escape. Then he reached to play with her clit. The little bundle of nerves was already swollen, and when he pressed his finger against it, she sucked in a sharp breath.

"Zachary!"

Hell and back. He loved the sound of his name in her mouth. And no matter how many times she screamed it, he'd never tire of hearing it.

He fucked her, tormented her, then moved faster and faster until her tiny whimpers became a solid never-ending cry for release.

"This is too much."

Her feminine heat squeezed him, demanding his orgasm in a mating ritual as old as time.

"I'm going to…" Gasping, she cried out, her wet pussy convulsing.

Though Zachary moved his hand away, he continued to hold her. While she shook her head, he traced his damp finger down the cleft of her ass.

"That was…" She fell silent, and he wondered if she was searching for the right word, or whether she wasn't thinking at all. "Indescribable."

"We're not done yet."

She exhaled a shuddering breath.

After untangling their heated bodies, he helped her to stand.

"You've almost worn me out."

"Almost? Then I need to work harder." Too impatient to wait, he swept her from her feet and carried her to the bed. Smartly she didn't protest, even when he joined her. "And now you're going to come on my face."

"But…" Frantically she shook her head.

"It's what I want." He plumped a pillow, then laid his head on it. "Get your sweet little ass over here and straddle my face." His eyes narrowed in warning. "Before you say anything, remember what I said about you making any negative comments about yourself."

"That's not—"

"Brace yourself on the headboard. I'm going to eat your pussy. We can argue all night, but I will prevail. You might as well get on with it."

Rather awkwardly, she placed her thighs on either side of his head. Her musky, sexually satisfied scent drove him wild. "Lower yourself onto me."

When she didn't react quickly enough, he pulled her down.

"Master Zachary!" She lifted herself up.

Holding her firmly, he licked her, back to front.

"Oh my *God.*" She gasped and jerked away.

"Last warning," he growled.

Her body shaking like it had the first night they played together, she whimpered.

Patience gone, he took control, moving her where he wanted so that he could insert two fingers into her pussy while pressing his thumb against her anus.

"This is…" Her knees trembled. "I've never experienced anything like this."

He tasted her, tongued her, savored her, and the more she relaxed, the more responsive she became. "Play with your breasts."

"Then I'll have to let go of the headboard."

"You don't want me to repeat myself."

"No. No, I don't, Sir."

Zachary moved his tongue faster, and she groaned. "Squeeze your nipples, tug on them, pinch them the way I would." He knew the moment she followed his order because she spread her thighs farther apart, resting her pussy on his face. *Perfect.*

Like a starving man, he ate her out until she came, drenching his face with her juices. Eventually he slowed his strokes and eased his fingers from inside her. "And now, *now* you're ready."

Driven by a primal alpha need to mark his woman, he tossed her beneath him without the consideration he usually granted.

Her eyes were wide, but no fear lurked in their depths.

"You're mine, Makenna. I'm going to make sure you accept it."

He grabbed her hands and yanked them over her head, pinning them against the mattress. Then he plowed into her pussy with one long, satisfying stroke.

In recognition of his power, her body yielded to his. Satisfied, he sucked in a breath. *"Fuck."* His entire life, he'd waited for this—for her. "Spread your legs." Though he was deep inside her channel, it wasn't nearly enough. He needed her complete capitulation. For a moment, he pulled out. "Lift your legs."

When she complied, he braced his shoulders on the backs of her knees and bore forward.

She gasped at the force of his penetration.

"Take all of me, Makenna." An image of her belly swollen with his child urged him on, both real and inevitable.

She called out his name, part plea, part desperation.

Finally his balls drew up. He groaned, unleashing the force of the orgasm he'd held back for weeks. "Jesus."

Moments later, spent, he rolled to the side, then pulled her toward him. With a heavy exhalation, she rested in his arms. Maybe she was recognizing the same thing that he was. This was forever.

⁂

"What is this?" Tightening the belt around her robe, Makenna walked into the living room.

Zachary—her lover—stood there, shirtless, wearing only a pair of casual pants, grinning as he poured a cup of coffee.

There were several silver carts lined up, all stacked with food.

"I figured you'd be hungry after last night, and I wasn't sure you'd even had time to eat dinner." He shrugged. "I had no idea what you'd like."

"So what did you do? Order the entire room service menu?"

"Pretty well. Crepes, waffles, bacon, eggs, toast, oatmeal, granola."

"And coffee?" She needed it.

When he suggested they have sex in front of the window, she'd been apprehensive. There were no other tall buildings nearby, so they couldn't be seen. But knowing he was watching made her tummy tumble. And then, when he'd made her look too... It had been beyond sexy. Their bodies moved together perfectly, and there had been unadulterated pleasure in his eyes, proving his attraction to her was real and honest. As they'd continued, her self-consciousness faded, and their lewd acts appealed to her own voyeuristic fantasies.

Afterward, they had dozed in each other's arms until he had gotten up out of bed to discard the condom, and he returned with a warm, damp cloth to soothe her tender nether region. A couple of times during the night, they made love before drifting gently back to sleep.

But now, in the light of day, anxiety gnawed at her happiness. Last night was over. And they both had to go back to their real lives. She might be emotionally changed, but he was still a billionaire playboy. Despite her resolve, she had become another notch on his bedpost.

"Makenna?" His head was tipped to the side quizzically, as if he'd been trying to get her attention.

"Sorry." She offered a quick smile. "I must be still half-asleep."

"Cream and sugar?"

"Just cream. Thanks." She walked across the room to accept the cup. "Manna from heaven."

He held it back until she kissed him.

Danger zone. From the moment they met, he'd encouraged her to remain in the moment. And as long as she did, things were fine, but when she looked to tomorrow or the next day, the future was bleak.

"What would you like to eat?" He removed the lids from the assorted plates.

"Maybe a little of everything." After all, he'd ordered a private buffet.

But instead of choosing anything healthy, she went straight for the crepes and covered them with strawberries and whipped cream. Then she snatched up a piece of bacon. "For protein."

He laughed. "Protein is good."

Once his plate was mounded with food, they moved to the dining room.

The blinds were lowered, but the sun still filtered through. "What time is it?"

"A little after ten. I needed to get up for a conference call with London."

"Sorry I slept so long."

"I wouldn't have blamed you if you'd stayed in bed until noon. In fact, we could both probably use the rest."

It had been a physically demanding night for him too.

"What would you like to do today?"

She put down her bacon without taking a bite. "I was planning to go home. Did you have a different idea?"

"I'm leaving town in the morning on business, but if you have no plans, we could be tourists in our own city."

The invitation caught her off guard. With his reputation, she'd expected he would take her home.

"Alternatively we could spend the day at the pool, have dinner after you get a massage." He grinned devilishly. "Or I could fuck you so hard you can't walk."

"Uh… The last part is already dangerously close to happening."

Greedily he perused her, taking in her mussed hair and the robe's gaping lapels that revealed her cleavage.

Since yesterday, her survival instincts had gone into hiding, and she ended up agreeing to spend the day together. "We can't stay out too late."

"I can take you home in the morning."

"You have a flight, and I am expected at the office by seven."

"I'll drop you off before I go to the airport."

More than anything, she wanted what he offered, even if it was dangerous. She had makeup in her bag, but she couldn't rewear yesterday's clothes. "I'd need a few personal items and maybe a sundress. And definitely a pair of shoes." Since she'd been meaning to buy some walking sandals, this was the perfect excuse.

"As you know, there's a shopping mecca attached to the resort."

Most with brands she'd never be able to afford.

"I'll go with you."

Her protests were ignored, not that she expected anything different.

Even though she took over an hour finalizing her purchases, he didn't check his watch or look at his phone, and he pulled out his credit card at every vendor.

"You don't need to do this."

"If I had let you go home, you wouldn't have needed all these things. Besides, Miss Ellie told me my crypto is still on the rise."

"Who am I to argue with that logic?" And honestly, it was nice to be spoiled. "You've been totally patient. I think your male complaint mode is defective."

He grinned. "I'll see if we can get Julien Bonds to install an upgrade."

As they took the private elevator back to PH2, as he called Penthouse Two, she couldn't resist her question. "You're friends with him?"

"With Bonds? Close enough."

Which meant… "He's a Titan."

"Are you referring to the organization that may or may not exist?"

The compartment arrived at the fifty-third floor so fast that her vertigo was triggered.

"The Bella Rosa believes in expediency. The quicker you get people to the casino floor, the better."

"I'll say."

Once they were back in his condo, she took a quick shower and got ready to go. He was dressed and doing some work in his office when she went looking for him.

"That dress is fabulous."

"Why, thank you." She twirled, and the hem flared a little.

"I'm going to wreck your hair before we leave."

Makenna gasped. "Are you serious?"

He pushed away from his desk and advanced toward her, eyes narrowed with purposeful intent. "As you know, there are certain things I don't joke about."

She stood her ground. "But I just—" Her breath whooshed out as he swept her off her feet and carried her to the bedroom.

"Since I'm a generous man, I'll allow you to keep your shoes on." He lowered her so she could put her feet on the floor.

With swift motions, he stripped her, then once again picked her up and placed her on the mattress, this time on all fours.

He rolled a condom down his thick shaft, then ensured she was ready for him before taking her from the rear.

When they were finished, she was overheated and dotted with perspiration. A quick glance in the bathroom mirror proved he had totally destroyed the bun she'd swept her hair into.

"Fair warning." Wearing only his trousers and a triumphant smile, his body gleaming from exertion, he stood behind her. "Seeing you all made-up ignites my inner beast." He pressed his cock against her.

In the mirror, she locked her gaze on him. "You're hard *again?*"

"You put your hair up." He shrugged fatalistically. "Of course, if you left it loose…" He swept the blonde locks aside to kiss the side of her neck. "Then I'll need to close my fist in it."

She shouldn't poke him. But she was caught up in her own tide of lust. "And do what?"

"This…" He caught a handful of hair at the root, firmly—just short of painfully—and pulled her head back. Then he kissed her…hard.

To remain upright she had to wrap her arms around his neck.

With his mouth, he claimed her completely, communicating something she was afraid to acknowledge.

When he finally released her, she grabbed hold of the vanity for support. "Thank you for the warning."

"Unless you want to spend the afternoon in my bed, I recommend you be at the front door in under two minutes." With that, he left.

She didn't point out that they would have already been at their first stop if he hadn't ripped off her clothes.

With a half shake of her head, she repaired the damage to her mascara and lipstick and did the best she could with her hair.

Once they were outside the casino, the Las Vegas heat blasted her.

Hand in hand, they wandered down the Strip, and she took in the sights that she normally missed because she was so busy working. When she visited a property, she paid cursory attention to the tigers or flamingos and instead spent her time evaluating the logistics of the meeting space. Some might enjoy dancing fountains as an amenity, but she wanted to know how responsive the catering staff was and if the manager was someone she could work with easily.

Because the day was growing hotter, they purchased bottles of water and continued their stroll, ending up at a resort that was featuring a showing of impressionist art.

"I'm so glad we came." On a normal Sunday, she'd be getting organized for the next week. If time permitted, she'd take a yoga class.

They stopped in front of the final painting. "This is absolutely amazing."

He nodded.

"There's all these wonderful things to do in Las Vegas. People come here from all over the world, and I've never been in this gallery before."

"We need to take the time to appreciate what we have."

She looked over at him, but he was still studying the work hanging on the wall.

"Next stop?" he asked eventually.

After buying ice cream sandwiches—a full scoop of butter pecan wedged between two chocolate chip cookies—they sat at a small metal table.

"How about a comedy club?"

"I've actually never been."

"Another thing I can corrupt you with." He opened an app and purchased tickets before booking early dinner reservations.

"I'd feel bad about the crepes and ice cream, but I think we've walked it off."

"There's no doubt."

At the restaurant, still quiet because it was relatively early, she opted for a Caesar salad with grilled chicken. He went straight for a steak and vegetables.

The stand-up comedians were superb.

Then, evening falling, they walked back on the other side of the street for a change of view. As he had all day, Zachary took her hand.

"I haven't done anything like this in forever." She savored the moment. "Thank you."

"We should plan another one soon."

By the time they reached his condo, her feet were throbbing, and she looked forward to soaking in the tub.

But he turned and narrowed his eyes. Her insides liquefied.

"I can pour you a glass of champagne. Or I can give you the spanking that you're craving."

All of a sudden, he was the masterful Dominant, rather than the solicitous man who'd spent the day catering to her every whim.

"Be mindful of your decision." His voice was roughened with command. "Because I'm inclined to give you forced orgasms if we play together."

"Fuck the champagne, Sir. I'll take a bottled water."

※

"Good morning, Mr. Denning and Makenna."

Miss Ellie's cheerful voice cut through Makenna's dreams, and she groaned. "Ten more minutes."

Zachary soothed her hair and kissed the top of her head.

"Please?" Last night, after he'd thoroughly spanked and fucked her, they'd agreed on a five a.m. wake-up call. It had seemed like a good idea. But that was before he'd made love to her two more times.

"I'll be back with coffee."

"With cream." She buried her head beneath the pillow, but without him in the bed, she couldn't go back to sleep.

With a resigned sigh, she tossed the blankets aside and padded into the bathroom. He was already in the walk-in shower, steam billowing around him, droplets of water sluicing down his sexy chest, and his cock magnificently hard.

Maybe sensing her presence, or hearing her gasp, he glanced over. "Join me?"

She knew better than to protest that it couldn't be done.

"Grab a condom?"

By the time she was back, he'd stepped out and toweled his lower body dry. Zachary rolled the condom down his shaft; then she followed him into the shower.

After kissing her, he turned her to face the wall, then reached around to play with her breasts and clit, ensuring she was turned on.

Once he was fully inside, he moved slowly, creating a sexy rhythm that made her wet. He kissed her neck and squeezed the ass he'd spent so much time tormenting last night.

When Makenna came, it wasn't with a huge shudder, but a soft, satisfied sigh.

"Lovemaking," he murmured.

She tipped back her head, and warm water trickled over her as he increased the force behind his thrusts until he came, gritting out her name in three distinct syllables.

Once they were done, he released her wrists. Still lethargic, she turned around. He tucked damp strands of hair behind her ears, then kissed her. "Now are you glad you didn't stay in bed?"

"Having sex with you is worth the lost sleep."

"Good." He lathered a bar of soap to wash her, and she luxuriated in every caress.

"I'm still going to need coffee."

"Miss Ellie has already brewed it."

"I think I love her."

"That's the nicest thing anyone has ever said to me. You could learn something, Mr. Denning."

Makenna laughed. "Can I take her home with me?"

"I shall make the inquiry of Mr. Bonds."

"Hell no." With his palm, Zachary wiped the water from his face. "I'll tell him to send you one."

By the time Makenna had finished her second cup, she was mostly awake, and running late.

Near the elevator, he stood waiting for her, freshly shaven, wearing a tailored suit, his addictive scent of power and spice branding the air.

Would he always have the ability to make her senses swim?

"Ready?"

"Don't you have a trip?" She looked around. "Where's your luggage?"

"I keep a full wardrobe and a complement of electronics on the jet."

Of course he had a private plane. *Who doesn't?*

"And my home in New York has everything I need."

In the same dizzying way that she'd never get used to, the elevator whisked them to the lobby. Outside, his snazzy yellow car was waiting, already purring. "You never have to wait." She, on the other hand, a mere mortal, spent half her life in frustrating lines.

"Miss Ellie notified the valet when she started the coffee."

"Wow. Again, I'm impressed."

Because traffic was light, he parked in front of her house five minutes ahead of his projected schedule.

"Thanks for the ride." She reached for the door handle but didn't pull it. "Have a successful trip."

One hand on the steering wheel, he angled his body toward her. "This is awkward."

A flutter of nerves teasing her, she asked, "What is?"

"I don't have your phone number."

She grinned. "That's ridiculous, isn't it?" Given the fact that she'd slept in his bed, and they'd had wet, steamy shower sex only an hour ago.

"I could track you down, but I don't want to call in any favors or put our friends in an awkward situation."

"Agreed."

He pulled out his Bonds device to program in her information. "You'll be hearing from me."

"I know you're busy." She hoped he meant it, but his dating history said otherwise. "Thanks for the weekend. It was nice." This time, she opened the door.

By the time she gathered her purse and the gym bag he'd loaned her for her purchases, he was standing beside her.

He walked her up the path. Once they were on the porch, he gathered her into his arms and kissed her in a way that curled her toes.

"That's a promise of things to come."

Her heart was thundering when she let herself inside, and she stood in the foyer until the purr of his car engine vanished into the predawn silence.

Then she straightened her shoulders. She had to put the fairytale fantasy of the weekend behind her.

Less than an hour later, Makenna was on the road. Because the caffeine she'd consumed wasn't nearly enough to power through this Monday morning, she drove through her favorite coffee place. She ordered their largest American for herself and a frozen chocolaty thing for Riley. And because she'd skipped breakfast, Makenna added pastries to the order.

As soon as she reached the first traffic light, she broke off a piece of maple nut scone and popped it in her mouth. Going to the gym after work was a small price to pay to indulge in such deliciousness.

About half an hour after she arrived at the office, her assistant swept in. Over coffee and their breakfast treats, they briefly chatted about their day off. Riley had gone to dinner with a friend. Makenna was vague about how she'd spent her time.

"But you had fun?"

"Yes. I did." Other than with Avery or Zara, Makenna wasn't willing to share any information about Master Zachary. "Ready to get to work?" She pulled up their joint calendar. "Can you meet Joelle and Nick at the cake-tasting appointment?" Attending food samplings was something she rarely did. But Joelle's mother was overly involved in the wedding preparation, so she wanted support with her at all times.

"No problem."

She assigned the appointment to Riley. "Good. I have a video pitch with a couple from Colorado today at two. This morning, I want to attend the preview of the new wedding chapel. Forget Elvis. You can choose about anything from a king to Merlin the magician." She laughed. "Only in Vegas."

"Can I go with you?"

"Why not? We can take a car together, but I'm heading from there to lunch with an event planner who's a bit miffed that we didn't consider them for the last tradeshow."

"Sounds like a plan." Riley brushed her hands together to wipe away the crumbs. "That was decadent." After a cheery wave, she vanished into her own office.

An hour before they were scheduled to leave, Riley knocked on the open door.

Makenna removed her reading glasses and looked up

from the spreadsheet she'd been studying. Riley's phone was clutched in her hand, and her cheeks were pale. "Is everything okay?"

"Can I come in?"

"Of course." Makenna frowned as Riley walked across the office.

"Have you…umm…" She extended her phone as she sank into a chair. "I think you need to see this."

"Okay." She accepted the device.

A picture of her and Zachary at the Rose Martini Bar leaped out. It had been snapped while he was kissing her hand. The headline was in all caps and bolded. FULL-FIGURED FABULOUSNESS. NEW ROMANCE FOR SIN CITY BILLIONAIRE?

A horrible roar echoed in her ears, and a headache slammed into her.

"God, Makenna. I'm so sorry."

With nerveless fingers, she scrolled down. The salacious words blurred together, and there were other pictures. Of course there was one of her taking a big bite from her ice cream sandwich. As if that wasn't bad enough, an arrow invited readers to discover the entire photo gallery.

Riley reached for the phone before Makenna dropped it.

"Are there more?"

"Yeah."

"Worse than that?"

"Makenna, look—"

"So, yes?" Her silence told Makenna all she needed to know. Her phone buzzed with an unknown number.

"Don't answer it."

She shouldn't have been surprised. After all, she'd seen pictures of his other conquests online. But now she understood the sickening invasion of privacy, knowing they'd been watched. And the comments on her weight...? The coffee she'd been drinking turned to acid.

The office phone rang, and automatically Riley answered with her customary cheerful greeting.

Makenna overheard enough to know it was a columnist seeking a comment. She shook her head and motioned for Riley to hang up.

"If you'd like to leave a message, I'll have Ms. Helton return your call when she's available."

On Makenna's desktop, her email chimed.

Trying to think, she squeezed her eyes shut. She'd never dealt with anything like this before and was at a loss.

Her cell phone rang again. "We'll let calls go to voicemail for the rest of the day. I'm sorry, but you'll need to listen to the messages so that we don't miss anything urgent. But we're not going to talk to the paparazzi." Another call shattered the silence. "This day is going to be awful."

When she'd first scened with Zachary, she'd known he was a player. But she'd had no idea that their relationship and her *full-figured fabulousness* were going to be laid bare for the entire world to muck around in.

Her phone lit up again, this time displaying Zachary's name. Her humiliation was complete. He'd obviously seen the same things she had—*Lots to Love. Thick is the New Thin.*

From the beginning, her intuition had warned her to stay away from him. But because of the fatal sexual attraction, she'd allowed herself to be seduced, and worse, to fall in love.

God. How could I have been so stupid?

She blinked back angry tears as she turned her phone facedown.

He called back two more times before sending a text.

DO NOT read the articles. They're trash.

. . .

Less than a minute later another message arrived.

I'm so fucking sorry, Makenna. This is on me. I should have thought to warn you that this might happen. You had a right to know what you were getting into.

The moment she finished reading, another appeared.

Call me.

Then a final one.

Please.

Aware of Riley watching her, Makenna shook her head. More than anything, this horrible experience had taught her one thing. She wasn't from his world, and she didn't belong in it. More than that, she wanted nothing to do with it.

"Do you want me to cancel your appointments?"

"No." She needed something to occupy her mind. Besides, some creeper had gotten a picture of her on the porch this morning. Which meant they knew where she lived. "I mean it's not like the whole world has seen the articles. Right?"

"Right."

Neither of them were convincing.

When she was alone again, she picked up her phone and

reread Zachary's messages. Then, her jaw set, her finger trembling, she typed in her response.

Don't ever contact me again.

And then, because she didn't trust herself not to weaken, she blocked his number.

CHAPTER SIX

God fucking damn it to hell. Zachary slammed his phone down. "Penny!"

With a polite smile, his flight attendant hurried over. "Yes, sir?"

"Let the pilot know I need to return home." No doubt there'd be a dozen details to attend to, but she was ultra-capable.

"Of course, Mr. Denning."

He picked up his phone to try Makenna's number again. Immediately it went to voicemail.

What the hell is she going through?

The constant speculation and harassment were the things he despised most about his life. The women he'd dated in the past had expected it; some had even thrived on having their names associated with his. But Makenna was different. *Innocent.* And this time the paparazzi had gone too far.

Since she was refusing his calls, he had no option but to do an internet search for her work number. And when he called that, he received an electronic greeting stating all lines were busy.

Shit.

In frustration, he sent several text messages. Thank God, he got a read receipt.

His next call was to the person who would help him coordinate the responses to the horrible articles—Celeste Fallon, a fellow Titan. Fallon and Associates had been in the PR and fixing business for well over a hundred years.

Despite the fact that he hadn't needed her services since his engagement ended, she picked up her private number on the first ring.

"Zachary. To what do I owe this pleasure?"

"It's not a fucking pleasure call."

"In that case, how can I help?"

"There's a young woman. And it's not what you're thinking." Her firm had dealt with some of the biggest scandals in history, events that had rocked the world and kept people glued to their televisions and computer screens. It was her job to change the conversation, and she was very good at it. "Nothing needs to be spun."

"I'm listening."

"Makenna Helton."

In the background, keys—presumably to Celeste's computer keyboard—clacked. "She's beautiful."

"She's mine."

"Generally you'd respond by saying no comment and letting it go."

"She's not from our world." She'd never been exposed to the nasty, relentless viciousness of the paparazzi, and they'd attacked her where she was most vulnerable. Zachary hated himself for bringing it down on her. "She's not going to know how to deal with this. I'm in the air right now, and…" He took a breath. "She won't take my calls."

"I'll reach out."

Maybe hearing from a woman would help. "I want the vultures kept away from her."

"Of course."

"I want the uncomplimentary goddamn disgusting articles removed. Not apologized for. Not retracted. Gone."

"That may take some time."

"Frankly, I don't care if you blow up the entire fucking internet." Because his world had been destroyed. He'd been attracted to her for months, and he'd cared about her since they'd first played. But over the weekend? He'd fallen in love. Completely, totally, making rational thought impossible.

"Zachary?"

He plowed his hand into his hair.

"I was asking for Ms. Helton's contact information."

He sent across her information. "As for her business number—"

"Already got it."

She was good. "Call *Scandalicious.*" They were a gossip site, but bigger and more reputable than most. "I'll give them an exclusive if they keep this shit off their front page."

"Consider it done."

He had no doubt she'd been deploying resources the entire time they'd been on the phone. She was as competent as she was efficient, and her network of people spanned the globe.

"I'm turning around and heading back home."

"I'll provide hourly updates, more often if warranted."

"Thanks, Celeste." Anger and agitation warred inside him, fighting for supremacy.

He'd done all he could for the moment, and he had to figure out how to harness his cold fury before he destroyed everything in his path.

A few minutes later, his phone pinged, and he grabbed it from his pocket and glanced at the screen.

Seeing Makenna's name, he sighed and opened the message.

Do not ever contact me again.

This time, her fuck-off was pointed. But it was going to take a hell of a lot more than that to make him stay away.

∞

Late in the day, the office door opened, and Makenna looked up, expecting to see Riley. Instead, two people—a man and a woman—entered the anteroom, and her heart thundered. *Press?* Wary, she stood and went to greet them. "Can I help you?"

"Ms. Helton?"

"Who's asking?"

The woman spoke first. "I'm Mira Araceli, and this is Torin Carter."

The tall, brooding man with electric eyes nodded.

"We're Hawkeye agents."

"Okay." She'd met Hawkeye at Cole and Avery's wedding, and she knew that Cole was associated with the security organization.

"We were told you were expecting us."

"No."

The pair exchanged glances.

"I'm confused. What can I do for you?" Surely they weren't here about an event.

"We were hired on behalf of Zachary Denning."

She pressed a finger to the bridge of her nose. "Look, I

think there's a mistake." She shook her head. "I don't need… whatever it is that you do."

Mira smiled warmly, easing Makenna's tension. "I'm sorry we caught you off guard. But our orders are clear. We'll be staying with you for an indefinite amount of time."

"I beg your pardon?" Mutinously, she folded her arms across her chest.

"The paparazzi can be aggressive."

"They're assholes, ma'am." Torin spoke for the first time. "That's a technical term."

Even though tension was swarming through her, she gave him a half smile. "At least we agree on one thing."

"Anyway, we're here to be sure no one takes pictures of you. And we also want to do a sweep of your neighborhood, including the sky. Some of them are using drone technology."

Makenna shivered.

It was almost quitting time, and it had crossed her mind that she might be followed. Looking over her shoulder all day while she'd been out on business had been nerve-racking.

In her skilled, reassuring way, Mira went on. "We know this isn't comfortable for you. We'll be with you during your workday and if you go out in the evenings. We'll pick you up and take you home. A surveillance team will work overnight at your house. We'll do our best to be as unobtrusive as possible."

As if Torin Carter could be unobtrusive. He was massive, and drop-dead gorgeous. If her guess was right, he was a Dominant—he had the air and bearing about him. "How long will this go on?"

"Until Mr. Denning gives us the all clear."

"And you have no idea when that might be?"

Torin spoke up again. "No, ma'am."

Even though she hated the intrusion in her life, she

appreciated Zachary's gesture, especially since she'd told him she never wanted to hear from him again.

"Do you have a garage door opener in your car?" Mira asked.

"I do."

"Good." Torin nodded. "Can we have the keys?"

As she handed them over, she gave them the make and model, along with the license plate number and location of the parking garage.

"No hurry, but let us know when you're ready."

She gathered her belongings, then answered a call from Zara.

"You okay?"

"It's, uhm… Stressful."

"You know they're haters, right? They intentionally use shitty angles to make their targets look bad. It's more sensational that way." She exhaled. "Everyone can see Zachary is besotted with you, and that makes the story clickbait. Don't let the trolls get to you. Pull your shoulders back and be a badass."

"Good advice." She just wished she could take it.

"Would you like me to come and stay with you?"

"That's really sweet." She hesitated to mention the security detail. "But I'm okay."

"You're absolutely beautiful, Kenna. And don't let anyone tell you otherwise. Promise you'll call if you need anything?"

"I swear."

"Let's go out for drinks after this blows over. You'll need a martini or two."

"Maybe three." After exchanging goodbyes, Makenna checked her office one last time before slinging her purse over her shoulder.

Torin outlined their strategy for moving her as quickly as

possible and instructed them to give him a thirty-second head start.

"You're doing great," Mira said. Then she opened an umbrella. "Stay under it and keep it low. It will make getting a decent snapshot impossible."

Outside, the rear car door stood open. Within seconds, she was in the passenger compartment, and Mira slid in after her. Simultaneously, Torin climbed into the driver's seat and pulled into traffic.

"This is surreal."

"Hopefully it's only for a day or so."

"How does this work with dinner and such?"

"If you want to order food, you can." As always, Mira was as soothing as she was practical. "But we'd like to ask for contactless delivery if you do."

Torin added his own opinion. "Assholes have been known to pretend to be florists, plumbers, delivery drivers."

She nodded. "Understood."

Mira shook her head. "While we'll have surveillance on you, we don't want to take unnecessary chances."

"Of course."

Later that evening, she grabbed a glass of wine and carried her tablet to the couch. Even though it was probably a very bad idea, she opened her web browser.

And now, even her favorite site, *Scandalicious,* had an article about her and Zachary. The headline sucked the breath from her lungs. SIN CITY'S FAVORITE BILLIONAIRE IS OFF THE MARKET!

Her hand shaking, she continued reading. *Billionaire banker Zachary Denning hasn't been seen much in recent months, and now we know why. He's been wining and dining a new love whose name is secret. And he sure looks happy.*

There were pictures, of course, but these were different.

Though they hadn't been retouched, the angles and lighting were better, and she didn't hate them.

Zara was right about the haters. And no doubt her words had come from experience.

Makenna took a drink before continuing, surprised to see Zachary quoted. In other articles, except business exposés, he always responded with, "No comment."

"She's beautiful on the inside and out, and I'm a lucky man. I don't deserve her. But I'm not going to stop trying."

She choked on a sob.

Though they were heartfelt, his words changed nothing. She refused to spend her life wondering who was lurking in the shadows, hoping to catch her looking awful.

After powering off the device, she went to take a bath. And then, sinking into the bubbles, she gave in to her tears.

The next day she was shocked to realize that all the articles—except the one in *Scandalicious*—had been removed from the internet. How was that even possible?

At the end of the week, Mira let Makenna know that their assignment was over, but they'd be back immediately if needed.

Which it won't be. Makenna was no longer in the spotlight. And though that was a welcome relief, being away from Zachary burned more than she could have imagined.

She went to the Hewitts' next party but left early when Zachary didn't attend.

A couple of weeks later, she returned to the office after lunch to find a massive bouquet on her desk.

She picked up the small, attached envelope to read the greeting.

Happy two-month anniversary.
I miss you.
Love, Zachary.

The constant ache in her heart accelerated into a throb.

The scent of the roses spiraled her back to Avery and Cole's wedding, and Zachary's words returned to haunt her, this time with more meaning. *"There comes a time when we have to stop letting our pain define who we are."*

For years, she'd done that—allowed her ex to ruin the way she saw herself.

She eased one of the flowers from the bunch. Unbidden, a memory returned to her—of Zachary and her having sex in his living room, and her being captivated by their reflection in the window.

To him, she was beautiful. His reaction was authentic. With both his words and actions, he'd repeatedly shown her how much he cared.

For too long, she'd allowed her ex's nasty words and unflattering paparazzi pictures to ruin her happiness.

Then she remembered the rest of what he'd said. *"When you're ready, I'll be here."*

Now, like before, he'd respected her need to be alone. And that made her fall even harder for him. Every day she'd looked but hadn't seen a single mention of him dating anyone else.

Their time apart hadn't damaged her affection for him. It had only increased it. She put down the rose and reread the card.

He'd signed it *Love.*

Did he mean it?

Life with Zachary, even with challenges, was better than life without him.

Her hand was shaking so hard that it took her two attempts to open the tab where she could unblock his number.

Because she wasn't brave enough to call him, she sent him a text message.

. . .

The flowers are beautiful.

The response took so long she wasn't sure that he would actually reply.

Dinner?

Her knees weakened. God, she'd missed him and ached to be with him.

I can send a car and bring you in via the private entrance. We can have dinner sent up to my place.

She considered that. But she refused to hide, even if photographers were lurking around. This was the new Makenna.

Actually I'd like to try out the steak house.

Eight o'clock? I'll make reservations.

The time dragged, and she was a nervous wreck by the time he met her at the hotel's private entrance and keyed her in.

Her breath caught. He was even more stunning than she remembered. His blue-gray eyes were dark, haunted, and his expression was stark. Though he was broad and strong, he looked as if he'd lost a few pounds that he didn't need to.

"Jesus, Makenna. I've fucking missed you." He pulled her into a small space just past the elevator and kissed her deeply, making her head spin and the ground ripple beneath her. "I was afraid this day would never come."

"I took your words to heart. I'm tired of letting my past define me."

"I'm so proud of you. But that was a fucking mess, and I'm sorry it happened."

She shook her head, and a tendril of hair curled alongside her face. "It's not your fault."

"I should have protected you better. Prepared you. Been more on guard." He raised his hands helplessly. "Something. I've kicked myself a million times, and I've slept with regret every night."

"I survived it. And learned to appreciate what I have. You said that to me at the art gallery."

"Makenna, my little innocent, I vow to always appreciate you."

They kissed again, only stepping apart when someone approached. "More later."

"Is that a promise?"

"It is."

Over a scrumptious meal, they caught up on the events of the past few weeks, and then the waiter rolled the dessert tray over. The sight of a slice of cheesecake topped with bittersweet chocolate made her mouth water.

"Have it," Zachary encouraged.

"I think I will." She nodded to the server. "With a cup of coffee."

"Very well. And for you, sir?"

"The same."

Once they'd finished dessert and were relaxing with their second cup of coffee, Zachary regarded her. "If you're amenable, I'd like you to stay the night."

She exhaled a great burst of relief. "I didn't bring a bag."

"We'll work something out. For what I have in mind, you won't need a lot of clothes. Can you take tomorrow off work?"

"Uhm…" She bit her lower lip. "Maybe I can talk my boss into it."

Since she was her own boss, he grinned. "Good. Because you're not going to get much sleep tonight. And I want to spend time getting reacquainted."

After he'd taken care of the bill, they headed for the elevator.

Her stomach lurched as the car whisked them upward. "I'd forgotten how fast this thing is."

"And I was hoping to be the one to sweep you off your feet."

In his living room, champagne was chilling in a tall silver ice bucket.

"Miss Ellie, close the blinds."

Nothing happened.

Makenna grinned. "Please, Miss Ellie."

"Why certainly, Makenna. My pleasure."

Zachary groaned. "I'm being ganged up on."

"If you remembered your manners, you'd be fine."

His eyes darkened, and he tipped back Makenna's chin. "I have other things on my mind."

"Oh?" Desire unfurled in her stomach.

He released her. "Champagne?"

"So… That means you are not planning to scene?"

"We have our whole lives in front of us, and I assure you, my little innocent, I certainly do intend to tie you up and paddle your delectable ass tomorrow. Tonight, however, is our anniversary. I want to make it memorable."

Her heart skipped a beat. "Every moment with you is

unforgettable." She yearned to be in his arms, sleeping next him, making love.

After tossing his suit coat on the back of the couch, he walked to the ice bucket to pour them both a glass.

"My beautiful Makenna." He offered her a flute, then raised his in a toast. "To the future. To you."

"To us." She'd only taken one sip when he took the drink from her and set it down alongside his on a nearby table.

"It's been… Unendurable. Worse than any battle I ever faced." His voice was raw, rubbed with emotion. "I miss you and can't go another day without you." He captured her, biting his fingers into the tender flesh of her upper arms, holding on as if he'd never let her go. He kissed her with more power than ever before, not just asking for her surrender, but demanding it. *"Fuck,* Makenna. I love you."

"You…"

"I love you. I've been losing my mind. There's never been anyone like you. From the moment I saw you watching the Hewitts, I knew you were mine."

"It took me a little longer to accept that."

He let her go to run his hand through his hair. "I'm screwing this up."

She placed a hand on his chest, over his heart. "What?"

Then her big powerful alpha lowered himself to one knee.

"Zachary?" She couldn't breathe.

"Will you…?" He reached into his pocket and pulled out a magnificent square-cut diamond ring. It winked in the light, casting its radiance everywhere. "Makenna Helton, will you do me the honor of becoming my bride?"

Emotion swamped over her as her dreams all came true. "Oh my God." She burst into tears.

"Makenna?" He remained where he was. "Put me out of my misery? Tell me you'll marry me."

"Yes, *yes."* Tears ran down her cheeks as he took her hand

in his and slid the ring into place. "A million times yes. I love you, Zachary. *I love you.*"

He stood and kissed her again, but this time there was a greater feeling to it. He tasted of promise. Of forever.

"It won't always be easy."

"We've had a glimpse of that."

"But together…? Turn to me, trust in me."

"Always." She raised on tiptoes to kiss him. "And forever."

∽

Makenna stretched out her legs and wiggled her toes, soaking in the warmth. For long minutes, she stared, taking in the stunning blue water of the Caribbean.

Zachary had been impatient and didn't want to wait to get married. Yesterday, just a week after he'd proposed, they'd had a small ceremony at the wedding chapel that she'd toured the day her life was turned upside down.

And he'd surprised her with a trip, booking them a private suite that overlooked the water. The villa's thatched roof added an island flair, and she was in love with the enormous four-poster bed. This morning, she'd been tempted to stay there all day.

But he'd coaxed her out with coffee and breakfast. And now they were lounging near the water and beneath a luxurious cabana that shaded them from the sun.

As an added benefit, they only had to share their server with one other couple.

"Most people call this a honeymoon. I call it a babymoon."

She tipped back the brim of her hat and lowered her sunglasses to look at him. "A babymoon is when a woman is pregnant and the couple takes a vacation before their child is born, like a last-chance getaway before giving birth."

"Well, that might be the traditional definition." He sipped

from the fruity drink that had been delivered in a coconut. It had all sorts of fruit on a dagger that crossed the opening, and it was adorned with a festive umbrella.

In any other man's hand, it might look ridiculous. But he was a breathtaking alpha.

"In our case, a babymoon is a trip we take for the express purpose of getting you pregnant."

"You…" Her book fell from her fingers.

He shrugged. "Or have fun trying."

"Are you serious?" Even though he was smiling, it appeared more like a king-of-the- mountain grin than actual humor.

"I am."

They'd talked about children in the abstract, but she hadn't realized that he'd meant now. Today, even.

"Any objection?"

"Uhm… A million, maybe."

"Let's hear them."

"Where will we live?"

"Anywhere you want. If you want a huge yard, we can have one. Doesn't have to be Vegas. We can go to LA or New York, even overseas." He stirred his drink.

"You've thought about this."

"My little innocent, that first night at my condo, I imagined your belly growing with my child. It was the most powerful orgasm of my life."

Her husband took her breath away.

"Next concern? In case you're worried, I'll be cutting back my travel schedule."

"Wait. What? You'll still be gone from time to time, right?"

"I'm offended." He took a long sip of the tropical-rum concoction. Then he raised a hand. "I solemnly swear I will not get in the way of your happy hours."

"Thank goodness." She leaned over and gave him a kiss. "That was my greatest worry."

"I knew it!"

"And…me working?"

"That's your call entirely. We can hire a nanny if needed. Or you can quit work if you want."

Makenna shook her head. "I love my job, and I've spent too long building the business just to walk away."

"Agreed."

"But maybe after we have a baby, I can work remotely sometimes."

"Or hire more staff."

"True." She had considered expanding, and Riley was definitely ready for more responsibility.

"Anything else?"

"That about covers it."

"Good, then we're set. You have a massage this evening. And dinner will be served at a private table for two near the ocean. And then we're going dancing."

"Really?"

"If you remember, once I had you on the dance floor at Cole and Avery's wedding, the band started playing, and I worked myself into your heart."

"That's not exactly true."

"No?"

"It was a little later." She grinned. "You had me at spearmint and eucalyptus."

His answering smile filled her soul. "So I did."

After they finished their drinks, he helped her up from her chaise longue. "How about an afternoon siesta?"

She narrowed her eyes suspiciously. "Why do I get the feeling your suggestion has nothing to do with sleep?"

"You could be right." He pulled her to him. "I love you, Makenna."

"And I love you, my protector, my lover…my Dominant."

He grabbed her rear and squeezed hard, igniting a flame. "Shall we?"

"After you, Sir."

◊ ◊ ◊ ◊ ◊

Thank you for reading Slow Burn. I hope you loved reading Makenna and Zachary's story. I loved the sexy set up and the way he broke through all of her barriers and insecurities. One reader asked me if Zachary had a brother! I'll tell you, he's the type of hero who really intrigues me. Loving, patient, able to see beyond society's expectations. I love him.

The Titans: Sin City series continues with All-In. Oh, my, my, my…maybe my sexiest story yet.

DISCOVER ALL-IN

And I've got some more, delicious alpha Titans billionaires that I'd like you to meet.

Rafe Sterling needs a bride, stat. But Rafe decides he wants Hope Malloy, the very woman hired to find him a bride. Trouble is, she doesn't date clients, and especially not one who is as terrifyingly alpha as the Sterling heir…

A ruthless Dominant billionaire marriage of convenience romance, with a touch of intrigue.

★★★★★ A flawless five-star read! ~New York Times Best Selling Author Angel Payne

DISCOVER BILLIONAIRE'S MATCHMAKER

Turn the page for an exciting excerpt from ALL-IN

ALL-IN
CHAPTER ONE

"Hey, boss. You need to have a look at this."

Lorenzo stopped on his way out of the security command center and strode back to the console where Enrico, one of his most trusted deputies, was seated. "What's up, Rico?"

Dozens of monitors supplied real-time video of Lorenzo's entire Bella Rosa resort, from the casino's numerous tables, to the hotel elevators, restaurants, nightclubs, food court, workout space, spa, even the numerous pool decks.

Rico selected one of the feeds, showing Excess, the nightclub.

The area was bathed in its signature purple light, and scores of Las Vegas's trendiest, richest were crowded onto the dance floor. The most expensive DJ in town spun tunes, and frenetic energy thumped through the place.

"This one, boss."

Lorenzo studied one of the monitors. A group of four people were being shown to their VIP table. "What am I looking at?" Or rather, *who?*

Rico zoomed in.

Fuck.

Even though she was faced away from him, and the long brunette sweep of her hair curtained around her in a glorious waterfall of distraction, Lorenzo knew her. His dick had cataloged her every sinful curve. Every primal instinct was on fire with the need to possess her.

Zara Davis.

What the hell was she thinking, venturing into the lethal grip of his lair? *Tempting fate?*

The rational part of his brain recognized that she was allowed to be here with anyone she wanted. He snarled. There'd never been anything rational about his reaction to the daughter of a man who owed a debt he was unable to repay.

After everyone was seated on the black leather couches, Zara's companion said something to her. She turned and gifted him with a smile so big and bright it would make ordinary men forget their names. And in this case, the lucky recipient was Maverick Rothschild, the spoiled son of one of America's richest families. Unaccountably the fact that she was dazzling the prick pissed Lorenzo the fuck off. "Shut it down."

"Sure, boss." Rico clicked a couple of buttons to resume his regular feed.

Throughout the day and evening, Lorenzo made regular sweeps through the public areas of his property—see and be seen. Which meant there was nothing unusual about leaving the room with Mario— his ever-present deputy—following close behind him.

Mario pressed his thumb to the unobtrusive pad that served as the private elevator's call button. This particular car existed solely for Lorenzo and his crew to move through the main tower without the annoyance of waiting.

They bypassed the line of people waiting behind the

velvet ropes to enter the nightclub and made their way through the throngs of revelers.

From the day the property opened, Excess had become one of Sin City's hottest spots. In that respect, it was no wonder Zara was here. Though she was an heiress, she'd distanced herself from her father and brothers and was charting her own path as a social media influencer. Her clients paid her big money to show up and be photographed at their events. But he'd never had any interest in being one of her clients.

He wanted much, much more from her.

Though he stopped to converse with a group of regulars, Lorenzo kept his eye on the VIP section. Zara was posed on the arm of the settee, head tipped back. The light caught the burnished copper in her hair, giving her an ethereal princess-like glow. The camera loved her. And maybe he did too.

He shook his head to clear it. *What the fuck?* Once again, there was nothing even remotely logical about his thought process—and hadn't been from the first time he'd seen her at her seventeenth birthday party.

Their server arrived with a bottle of whiskey and cocktails, sliding them onto the glass-topped table.

The Rothschild spawn took her wrist and tugged her down onto the cushion next to him.

Leashing his possessive anger, Lorenzo threaded his way toward their table. No doubt she knew he'd had eyes on her since she walked through the building's main entrance. But he wanted her to know how closely he was watching.

Their other guests headed out to the dance floor, leaving her alone with Rothschild. While she reached into her purse for a tube of lipstick, fucking Rothschild tipped a powder into her drink. When she faced him again, he picked up the martini glass and offered it to her.

Fury flamed. "Move in."

Behind him, Mario cued his comms and began issuing instructions to the security staff.

Predator to prey, hands clenched at his sides, Lorenzo devoured the remaining distance. To her, he snapped, "Put down that glass," then he yanked Rothschild to his feet.

"Lorenzo!"

His fury focused, he landed a satisfying uppercut to the little fucker's jaw, sending him reeling back onto the couch. Mario moved in closer, and two other men arrived, blocking sightlines while providing their boss with the protection he needed.

When Lorenzo's vision cleared, Zara was standing there, hands on her hips, eyes blazing with regal indignation. "What the hell are you doing, Lorenzo?"

"Saving your ass."

"I'm capable of taking care of myself."

The fuck you are. "Get him out of here."

Mario hauled Rothschild to his feet again. Wobbling, he rubbed his jaw.

Lorenzo got in the man's face and smelled the putrid stench of fear. "Either walk under your own power like the man you pretend to be, or you'll be carried out of here on a gurney."

"The hell is wrong with you? I didn't do anything." A lock of hair fell forward, making him look like a petulant toddler.

"If she took even one sip, they'll never find your worthless body."

Rothschild's remaining color fled, and he might have crumpled if Mario hadn't been behind him.

"This time your daddy isn't going to be able to save you, you sorry motherfucker."

Zara grabbed Lorenzo's forearm. "Stop being a Neanderthal." Then, shaking her head, she looked at her date again. "Maverick? Are you okay?"

"He has nothing to say to you." Or wouldn't, if he was smart. Lorenzo angled his head toward Mario and two other security members. "Save a piece of him for me. Move."

"Lorenzo!" She squeezed his arm tighter. "You can't do this."

"If you know what's good for you, *principessa,* keep your mouth shut."

"This is outrageous, and I will not be told what—"

"Oh yes." He leaned in closer, breathing in the life-giving scent of her, innocence mixed with feminine allure. "You will."

Without anyone being aware of what was happening, the trio of his men escorted Rothschild through an unseen exit. He'd have plenty of time to think before Lorenzo arrived to deliver the rest of his punishment.

Then he turned his full attention on Zara. "You're with me."

As she released her grip, she shook her head, her eyes spiking with hard daggers. "Who the hell do you think you are?"

"The lord and master of all I survey." He raked his gaze down her body. *Jesus fucking Christ.* She didn't have a bra on underneath the little black silver number she wore.

If he didn't get her out of here in the next few seconds, he'd lose what was left of his composure. "Let's go, Zara."

"Absolutely not." She shook her head. "We came with friends, and I'm not leaving without Mav."

"You can see what's left of him tomorrow." It was a lie. After tonight, Maverick Rothschild would never look at—or talk to—her again.

"I mean it, Lorenzo."

He picked up her purse, zipped it open, then pulled out her cell phone. "Pass code?"

"Screw you."

He offered it to one of his team. "Break in."

"Wait!"

Lorenzo regarded her.

"It's biometric."

He reached for her hand and pressed her fingertip to the scanner. Once it was unlocked, he glanced at her again. "Who are you here with?"

"Elias Henry." She gritted her teeth. "A client who is paying me big money, and the woman he's trying to impress."

"They'll enjoy their evening." He typed in a message and then dropped the device back into her purse.

The server passed by, and he stopped her. "Let Mr. Henry know his bill is comped and that he has a table available at the steak house anytime he wishes."

Zara's mouth fell open, and the sight was satisfying.

"Get rid of these drinks and bring fresh ones."

"Of course, sir."

"If there are no other objections, Ms. Davis, please come with me."

She stood her ground. He admired her defiance, as useless as it was. It made the next few seconds even more satisfying. "I'm not open to discussion or compromise." He leaned in, crowding her space, and spoke softly. "You can come with me willingly, or I'll toss you over my shoulder." Did she have any fucking clue how much his inner alpha male wanted to goad her into taking the second option? "What will people say when they see pictures of your ass in the air?" Especially since his hand would be on it.

She went pale. He had a certain reputation, and she knew it. "Lorenzo—"

"Choose, *principessa*. And do it now."

ABOUT THE AUTHOR

I invite you to be the very first to know all the news by subscribing to my very special VIP Reader newsletter! You'll find exclusive excerpts, bonus reads, and insider information.

https://www.sierracartwright.com/subscribe/

For tons of fun and to join with other awesome people like you, join my reader group here:

https://www.facebook.com/groups/SierrasSuperStars

International bestselling author Sierra Cartwright was born in England, and she spent her early childhood traipsing through castles and dreaming of happily-ever afters. She was raised in Colorado and now calls Galveston, Texas home. She loves to connect with her readers, so please feel free to drop her a note.

ALSO BY SIERRA CARTWRIGHT

Titans

Sexiest Billionaire

Billionaire's Matchmaker

Billionaire's Christmas

Determined Billionaire

Scandalous Billionaire

Relentless Billionaire

Titans Quarter

His to Claim

His to Love

His to Cherish

Titans Sin City

Hard Hand

Slow Burn

All-In

Hawkeye

Come to Me

Trust in Me

Meant For Me

Hold On To Me

Believe in Me

Bonds

Crave

Claim

Command

Donovan Dynasty

Bind

Brand

Boss

Mastered

With This Collar

On His Terms

Over The Line

In His Cuffs

For The Sub

In The Den

Collections

Titans Series

Titans Billionaires: Firsts

Titans Billionaires: Volume 1

Hawkeye Series

Here for Me: Volume One

Printed in Great Britain
by Amazon